George Barr McCutcheon

What's-His-Name

George Barr McCutcheon

What's-His-Name

1st Edition | ISBN: 978-3-75243-722-5

Place of Publication: Frankfurt am Main, Germany

Year of Publication: 2020

Outlook Verlag GmbH, Germany.

What's-His-Name

BY

GEORGE BARR McCUTCHEON

WITH ILLUSTRATIONS BY

HARRISON FISHER

NEW YORK

GROSSET & DUNLAP

PUBLISHERS

CHAPTER I

OUR HERO

Two men were standing in front of the Empire Theatre on Broadway, at the outer edge of the sidewalk, amiably discussing themselves in the first person singular. It was late in September and somewhat early in the day for actors to be abroad, a circumstance which invites speculation. Attention to their conversation, which was marked by the habitual humility, would have convinced the listener (who is always welcome) that both had enjoyed a successful season on the road, although closing somewhat prematurely on account of miserable booking, and that both had received splendid "notices" in every town visited.

These two loiterers serve a single purpose in this tale—they draw your attention to the principal character, to the person who plays the title rôle, so to speak, and then, having done so, sink back into an oblivion from which it is quite unnecessary to retrieve them.

The younger of the two players was in the act of lighting a cigarette, considerately tendered by the older, when his gaze fell upon the figure of the approaching hero. He hesitated for a moment, squinting his eyes reflectively as if to make sure of both vision and memory before committing himself to the declaration that was to follow.

"See that fellow there? The little chap with his hands in his pockets?"

The other permitted a vague, indifferent glance to enter the throng of pedestrians, plainly showing that he did not see the person indicated. (Please note this proof of the person's qualifications as a hero.)

"The fellow in front of Browne's," added the first speaker, so eagerly that his friend tried once more and succeeded.

"What of him?" he demanded, unimpressed.

"That is What's-His-Name, Nellie Duluth's husband."

The friend's stare was prolonged and incredulous.

"That?"

"Yes. That's the fair Nellie's anchor. Isn't he a wonder?"

The object of these remarks passed slowly in front of them and soon was lost in the crowd. Now that we know who he is we will say thank you to the obliging Thespian and be off up Broadway in his wake, not precisely in the capacity of spies and eavesdroppers, but as acquaintances who would know him better.

He was not an imposing figure. You would not have looked twice at him. You could not have remembered looking once at him, for that matter. He was the type of man who ambles through life without being noticed, even by those amiably inclined persons who make it their business to see everything that is going on, no matter how trivial it is.

Somewhere in this wide and unfeeling world the husband of Nellie Duluth had an identity of his own, but New York was not the place. Back in the little Western town from which he came he had a name and a personality all his own, but it was a far cry from Broadway and its environments. For a matter of four or five years he had been known simply as "Er—What's-His-Name? Nellie Duluth's husband!" You have known men of his stripe, I am sure; men who never get anywhere for the good and sufficient reason that it isn't necessary. Men who stand still. Men who do not even shine by reflected glory. Men whose names you cannot remember. It might be Smith or Brown or Jones, or any of the names you can't forget if you try, and yet it always escapes you. You know the sort I mean.

Nellie Duluth's husband was a smallish young man, nice-looking, even kind-looking, with an habitual expression of inquiry in his face, just as if he never quite got used to seeing or being seen. The most expert tailor haberdasher could not have provided him with apparel that really belonged to him. Not that he was awkward or ill-favoured in the matter of figure, but that he lacked individuality. He always seemed to be a long way from home.

Sometimes you were sure that he affected a slight, straw-coloured moustache; then, a moment afterward, if you turned your back, you were not quite sure about it. As a matter of fact, he did possess such an adornment. The trouble came in remembering it. Then, again, his eyes were babyish blue and unseasoned; he was always looking into shop windows, getting accustomed to the sights. Trolley cars and automobiles were never-decreasing novelties to him, if you were to judge by the startled way in which he gazed at them. His respect for the crossing policeman, his courtesy to the street-car conductor, his timidity in the presence of the corner newsboy, were only surpassed by his deference to the waiter in the cheap restaurants he affected.

But, ah! You should have seen him in that little Western town! He was a "devil of a fellow" out there! He knew the policemen by their first names and had no respect for them; street-car conductors were hail-fellows well met, and the newsboys wore spectacles and said "Yes, sir," to him. As for the waiters, he knew them all by their Christian name, which usually was Annie or Mamie or Katie.

On Broadway he was quite another person. He knew his Broadway from one end to the other—that is to say, he knew that side of the "Great White Way" which stares you in the face and rebukes you for staring back—the outside of Broadway. He had been on and off Broadway for a matter of five years and yet he had never recovered from the habit of turning out for every pedestrian he met, giving the other man the right of way instead of holding to his own half of it, sometimes stepping in puddles of water to do so and not infrequently being edged off the curbstone by an accumulation of the unexpected.

Once in a while during his peregrinations some one recognised him and bowed in a hesitating manner, as if trying to place him, and at such times he responded with a beaming smile and a half-carried-out impulse to stop for a bit of a chat, but always with a subsequent acceleration of speed on discovering that the other fellow seemed to be in a hurry. They doubtless knew him for Miss Duluth's husband, but for the life of them they couldn't call him by name. Every one understood that Nellie possessed a real name, but no one thought to ask what it was.

Moreover, Nellie had a small daughter whose name was Phoebe. She unquestionably was a collaboration, but every one who knew the child spoke of her as that "darling little girl of Nellie's." The only man in New York who appeared to know Nellie's husband by name was the postman, and he got it second-hand.

At the stage door of the theatre he was known as Miss Duluth's husband, to the stage hands and the members of the chorus he was What's-His-Name, to the principals he was "old chap," to Nellie herself he was Harvey, to Phoebe he was "daddy," to the press agent he was nameless—he didn't exist.

You could see Nellie in big red letters on all the billboards. She was inevitable. Her face smiled at you from every nook and corner—and it was a pretty face, too—and you had to get your tickets of the scalpers if you wanted to see her in person any night in the week, Sundays excepted. Hats, parasols, perfumes, and face powders were named after her. It was Nellie here and Nellie there and Nellie everywhere. The town was mad about her. It goes without saying that her husband was not the only man in love with her.

As Harvey—let me see—oh, never mind—What's-His-Name—ambled up Broadway on the morning of his introduction into this homely narrative he was smiled at most bewitchingly by his wife—from a hundred windows—for Nellie's smile was never left out of the lithographs (he never missed seeing one of them, you may be sure)—but it never occurred to him to resent the fact that she was smiling in the same inviting way to every other man who looked.

He ambled on. At Forty-second Street he turned to the right, peering at the curtained windows of the Knickerbocker with a sort of fearful longing in his mild blue eyes, and kept on his way toward the Grand Central Station. Although he had been riding in and out of the city on a certain suburban train for nearly two years and a half, he always heaved a sigh of relief when the gate-tender told him he was taking the right train for Tarrytown. Once in a great while, on matinée days, he came to town to luncheon with Nellie before the performance. On Sundays she journeyed to Tarrytown to see him and Phoebe. In that way they saw quite a bit of each other. This day, however, he was taking an earlier train out, and he was secretly agitated over the possibility of getting the wrong one. Nellie had sent word to the theatre that she had a headache and could not have luncheon with him.

He was not to come up to her apartment. If he had known a human being in all New York with whom he could have had luncheon, he would have stayed in town and perhaps gone to a theatre. But, alas, there was no one! Once he had asked a low comedian, a former member of Nellie's company, but at the time out of a job and correspondingly meek, to luncheon with him at Rector's. At parting he had the satisfaction of lending the player eleven dollars. He hoped it would mean a long and pleasant acquaintance and a chance to let the world see something of him. But the low comedian fell unexpectedly into a "part" and did not remember Nellie's husband the next time he met him. He forgot something else as well. Harvey's memory was not so short. He never forgot it. It rankled.

He bought a noon extra and found a seat in the train. Then he sat up very straight to let people see that they were riding in the same car with the great Nellie Duluth's husband. Lucky dog! Every one was saying that about him, he was sure. But every one else had a noon extra, worse luck!

After a while he sagged down into the seat and allowed his baby-blue eyes to fall into a brown study. In his mind's eye he was seeing a thousand miles beyond the western bank of the Hudson, far off into the quiet streets of a town that scarcely had heard the name of Nellie Duluth and yet knew him by name and fame, even to the remotest nook of it.

They were good old days, sweet old days, those days when he was courting her—when she was one among many and he the only one. Days when he could serve customers in his shirt-sleeves and address each one familiarly. Every one was kind. If he had a toothache, they sympathised with him and advised him to have it pulled and all that sort of thing. In New York (he ground his teeth, proving that he retained them) no one cared whether he lived or died. He hated New York. He would have been friendly to New York—

5

cheerfully, gladly—if New York had been willing to meet him halfway. It was friendly to Nellie; why couldn't it be friendly to him? He was her husband. Why, confound it all, out in Blakeville, where they came from, he was somebody while she was merely "that girl of Ted Barkley's." He had drawn soda water for her a hundred times and she had paid him in pennies! Only five years ago. Sometimes she had the soda water charged; that is to say, she had it put on her mother's bill. Ted couldn't get credit anywhere in town.

And now look at her! She was getting six hundred dollars a week and spurned soda water as if it were poison.

His chin dropped lower. The dreamy look deepened.

"Doggone it," he mused for the hundredth time, "I could have been a partner in the store by this time if I'd stuck to Mr. Davis."

He was thinking of Davis' drug store, in Main Street, and the striped blazer he wore while tending the soda fount in the summer time. A red and yellow affair, that blazer was. Before the "pharmacy law" went into effect he was permitted to put up prescriptions while Mr. Davis was at meals. Afterward he was restricted to patent medicines, perfumes, soaps, toilet articles, cigars, razor strops, and all such, besides soda water in season. Moreover, when circuses came to town the reserved-seat sale was conducted in Davis' drug store. He always had passes without asking for them.

Yes, he might have been a partner by this time. He drew a lot of trade to the store. Mr. Davis could not have afforded to let him go elsewhere.

Five years ago! It seemed ages. He was twenty-three when he left Blakeville. Wasted ages! Somehow he liked the ready-made garments he used to buy at the Emporium much better than those he wore nowadays—fashionable duds from Fifth Avenue at six times the price. He used to be busy from seven A.M. till ten P.M., and he was happy. Nowadays he had nothing to do but get up and shave and take Phoebe for walks, eat, read the papers, tell stories to Phoebe, and go to bed. To be sure, the food was good and plentiful, the bed was soft, and the cottage more attractive than anything Blakeville could boast of; Phoebe was a joy and Nellie a jewel, but—heigh-ho! he might have been a partner in Davis' drug store if he'd stayed in the old town.

The man in the seat behind was speaking to him. He came out of his reverie with a glad rush. It was so unusual for any one to take the initiative that he was more than ready to respond.

"I see the Giants lost again yesterday," said the volunteer conversationalist.

"Yes. Six to four," said our hero, brightly, turning in his seat. He always read the baseball news. He could tell you the batting average of every player in the big leagues for ten years back.

"Lot of bone-heads," said the other sourly. At first glance our friend thought he looked like an actor and his heart sank. But perhaps he might be a travelling salesman. He liked them. In either event, the stranger's estimate of the New York ball team pleased him. He rejoiced in every defeat it sustained, particularly at the hands of the Chicagos.

"Not in it with the Cubs," he announced, blitheness in his manner. Here was a man after his own heart.

But the stranger glared at him. "The Cubs?" he said, his voice hardening, his manner turning aggressive.

"They make the Giants look like two-spots," went on our friend, recklessly.

The stranger looked him over pityingly and then ended the conversation by deliberately hiding himself behind his newspaper. Our hero opened his lips to add further comment, but something in the way the paper crackled caused him to close them and turn back to his bitter survey of the Hudson. And the confounded fellow had invited his confidence, too!

He got down at Tarrytown and started up the hill. The station-master pointed him out to a friend.

"That's—er—What's-His-Name—Nellie Duluth's husband."

"That guy?"

"She keeps him up here in a cottage to take care of the baby. Away from the temptations of the city," said the agent, with a broad wink.

"I didn't know she was married," said his friend, who lived in Yonkers.

"Well, she is."

Mr.—(I declare, his name escapes me, so I will call him by his Christian name, Harvey)—Harvey, utterly oblivious to the pitying scrutiny of the two men, moved slowly up the road, homeward bound. He stopped in the middle of the sidewalk to light a "Sweet Cap," threw back his unimposing shoulders, and accelerated his gait a trifle in deference to his position as the master of a celebrity.

It was his habit to take a rather roundabout way up to the little cottage on the hill. The route led him past a certain drug store and a grocer's where he was on speaking terms with the clerks. They knew him. He did the marketing, but the account was in Miss Duluth's name. A livery stable, too, was on the line of progress. He occasionally stopped in to engage a pony phaeton for a drive in the afternoon with Phoebe.

7

To-day he passed these places by. Every one seemed to be busy. He could see that at a glance. So there wasn't any use stopping. That was what he got for coming home from town in the middle of the day. He nodded to several acquaintances—passing acquaintances in both senses of the word. They turned to look after him, half-smiles on their lips.

One woman said to another, "I wonder if he's really married to her?"

"If he wasn't, he'd be living in the city with her," was the complete rejoinder.

"He seems such a quiet little man, so utterly unlike what a husband of hers ought to be. He's from the far West—near Chicago, I believe. I never can remember his name. Can you?"

"I've never heard it."

"It's not an uncommon name."

"Why doesn't he call himself Mr. Duluth?"

"My husband says actresses are not supposed to have husbands. If they have them, they keep them in the background."

"That's true. I know I am always surprised when I see that they're trying to get divorces."

Harvey was never so far in the background as when he appeared in the foreground. One seldom took notice of him unless he was out of sight, or at least out of hearing.

He was not effeminate; he was not the puerile, shiftless creature the foregoing sentences may have led you to suspect. He was simply a weakling in the strong grasp of circumstance. He could not help himself; to save his life, he could not be anything but Nellie Duluth's husband.

Not a bad-looking chap, as men of his stamp go. Not much of a spine, perhaps, and a little saggy about the shoulders; all in all, rather a common type. He kept his thin moustache twisted, but inconsistently neglected to shave for several days—that kind of a man. His trousers, no matter how well made, were always in need of pressing and his coat was wrinkled from too much sitting on the small of his back. His shirts, collars, and neckties were clean and always "dressy." Nellie saw to that. Besides he always had gone in for gay colours when it came to ties and socks. His watch-fob was a thing of weight and pre-eminence. It was of the bell-clapper type. In the summer time he wore suspenders with his belt, and in the winter time he wore a belt with his suspenders. Of late he affected patent-leather shoes with red or green tops; he walked as if he despised the size of them.

Arriving at the snug little cottage, he was brought face to face with one of the common tragedies of a housekeeper's life. The cook and the nursemaid, who also acted as waitress and chambermaid, had indulged in one of their controversies during his absence, and the former had departed, vowing she would never return. Here it was luncheon time and no one to get it! He knew that Bridget would be back before dinner time—she always did come back—but in the meantime what were they to do? There wasn't a thing in the house.

He found himself wishing he had stayed in the city for luncheon.

Annie's story was a long one, but he gathered from it that Bridget was wholly to blame for the row. Annie was very positive as to that.

"Have we any eggs?" asked the dismayed master.

"Eggs? How should I know, sir?" demanded Annie. "It's Bridget's place to know what's in the pantry, not mine. The Lord knows I have enough to do without looking after her work."

"Excuse me," said he, apologetically. He hesitated for a moment and then came to a decision. "I guess I'd better go and see what we've got. If we've got eggs, I can fry 'em. Bridget will be back this evening."

"I'm not so sure of that," said Annie, belligerently. "I told her this was the last time, the very last."

"I'll bet you a quarter she comes back," said he, brightly.

"Gee! What a sport you are!" scoffed Annie.

He flushed. "Will you please set the table?"

"It's set."

"Oh!"

"I'll help you make the toast, if you'd like," said she, a sudden feeling of pity for him coming into her niggardly soul.

"Thanks," he said, briskly. "And the tea, too?"

"I think we'd better have coffee," said she, asserting a preference for the housemaid's joy.

"Just as you say," he acquiesced, hastily. "Where is Phoebe?"

"Next door with the Butler kids—children, I mean. Maybe they'll ask her to stay to lunch."

He gave her a surprise. "Go over and tell her to come home. I don't want her staying to luncheon with those damned Butlers."

She stared, open-mouthed. "I'm sure, sir, they're quite as good as—as we are.

What have you got against 'em?"

He could not tell her that Butler, who worked in a bank, never took the trouble to notice him except when Nellie was out to spend Sunday.

"Never mind. Go and get Phoebe."

He made a dash for the kitchen, and when the exasperated Annie returned a few minutes later with Phoebe—rebellious Phoebe, who at that particular moment hated her father—he was in his shirt-sleeves and aproned, breaking eggs over a skillet on the gas stove. His face was very red, as if considerable exertion had been required.

Phoebe was pouting when she came in, but the sight of her father caused her to set up a shriek of glee.

"What fun, daddy!" she cried. "Now we'll never need Bridget again. I don't like her. You will be our cook, won't you?"

Annie's sarcastic laugh annoyed him.

"I used to do all the cooking when the Owl Club went camping," he announced, entirely for Annie's benefit.

"In Blakeville?" asked Annie, with a grin.

"Yes, in Blakeville," he exploded, almost dropping the cigarette from his lips into the skillet. His blue eyes flashed ominously. Annie, unused to the turning of the worm, caught her breath.

Suddenly obsessed by the idea that he was master in his own house, he began strutting about the kitchen, taking mental note of the things that needed attention, with a view to reproving Bridget when she came back to the fold. He burnt his fingers trying to straighten the stovepipe, smelt of the dish-cloths to see if they were greasy, rattled the pans and bethought himself of the eggs just in the nick of time. In some haste and embarrassment he removed the skillet from the fire just as Annie came out of the pantry with the bread and the coffee can.

"Where's the platter?" he demanded, holding the skillet at arm's length. "They're fried."

"They'll be stone cold," said she, "waiting for the coffee to boil. You ain't got any water boiling."

"I thought, perhaps, we'd better have milk," he said, gathering his wits.

To his surprise—and to her own, for that matter—she said, "Very good, sir," and repaired to the icebox for the dairy bottles. He was still holding the skillet when she returned. She was painfully red in the face.

Phoebe eyed the subsequent preparations for the meal with an increasing look of sullenness in her quaint little face. She was rather a pretty child. You would say of her, if you saw her in the street, "What a sweet child!" just as you would say it about the next one you met.

Her father, taking note of her manner, paused in the act of removing his apron.

"What's the matter, darling?"

"Can't I go over to Mrs. Butler's for luncheon?" she complained. "They're going to have chicken."

"So are we," said he, pointing to the eggs.

"I want to go," said Phoebe, stubbornly.

He coloured. "Don't you want to stay home and eat what daddy has cooked?" he asked, rather plaintively.

"I want to go."

He could only resort to bribery. "And daddy'll take you down to see the nickel show as soon as we've finished," he offered. The child's face brightened.

Here Annie interposed.

"She can't go to see them nickel shows; Miss Duluth won't stand for it. She's give me strict orders."

"I'll take good care of her——" began Phoebe's father.

"Miss Duluth's afraid of diphtheria and scarlet fever," said Annie, resolutely, as she poured out a glass of milk for him.

"Not likely to be any diphtheria this time of year," he began again, spurred by the kick Phoebe planted on his kneecap.

"Well, orders is orders. What Miss Duluth says goes."

"Ah, come now, Annie——"

"Say, do you want her to ketch scarlet fever and die?" demanded the nurse, putting the bottle down and glaring at him with a look of mixed commiseration and scorn.

"Good Heavens, no!" he ejaculated. The very thought of it brought a gush of cold water to his mouth.

"Well, take her to see it if you must, but don't blame me. She's your kid," said Annie, meanly, with victory assured.

"Make her say 'Yes,'" urged Phoebe, in a loud whisper.

He hedged. "Do you want to have the scarlet fever?" he asked, dismally.

"Yes," said Phoebe. "And measles, too."

The sound of heavy footsteps on the back porch put an end to the matter for the time being. Even Phoebe was diverted.

Bridget had come back. A little ahead of her usual schedule, too, which was food for apprehension. Usually she took the whole day off when she left "for good and all." Never before in the history of her connection with Miss Duluth's menage had she returned so promptly. Involuntarily the master of the house glanced out of the window to see if a rain had blown up. The sun was shining brightly. It wasn't the weather.

The banging of the outer door to the kitchen caused him to jump ever so slightly and to cast a glance of inquiry at Annie, who altered her original course and moved toward the sitting-room door. In the kitchen a perfectly innocent skillet crashed into the sink with a vigour that was more than ominous.

A moment later Bridget appeared in the door. She wore her best hat and gloves and the dress she always went to mass in. The light of battle was in her eye.

"We—we thought we wouldn't wait, Bridget," said Mr.—er—What's-His-Name, quickly. "You never come back till six or seven, you know, so—"

"Who's been monkeyin' wid my kitchen?" demanded Bridget. She started to unbutton one of her gloves and the movement was so abrupt and so suggestive that he got up from his chair in such a hurry that he overturned it.

"Somebody had to get lunch," he began.

"I wasn't sp'akin' to you," said Bridget, glaring past him at Annie.

He gulped suddenly. For the second time that day his eyes blazed. Things seemed to be dancing before them.

"Well, I'm speaking to you!" he shouted, banging the table with his clenched fist.

"What!" squealed Bridget, staggering back in astonishment.

He remembered Phoebe.

"You'd better run over to the Butlers', Phoebe, and have lunch," he said, his voice trembling in spite of himself. "Run along lively now."

Bridget was still staring at him like one bereft of her senses when Phoebe scrambled down from her chair and raced out of the room. He turned upon the cook.

"What do you mean by coming in here and speaking to me in that manner?" he demanded, shrilly.

"Great God above!" gasped Bridget weakly. She dropped her glove. Her eyes were blinking.

"And why weren't you here to get lunch?" he continued, ruthlessly. "What do we pay you for?"

Bridget forgot her animosity toward Annie. "What do yez think o' that?" she muttered, addressing the nursemaid.

"Get back to the kitchen," ordered he.

Cook had recovered herself by this time. Her broad face lost its stare and a deep scowl, with fiery red background, spread over her features. She imposed her huge figure a step or two farther into the room.

"Phat's that?" she demanded.

She weighed one hundred and ninety and was nearly six feet tall. He was barely five feet five and could not have tipped the beam at one hundred and twenty-five without his winter suit and overcoat. He moved back a corresponding step or two.

"Don't argue," he said, hurriedly.

"Argue?" she snorted. "Phy, ye little shrimp, who are you to be talkin' back to me? For two cents I'd—"

"You are discharged!" he cried, hastily putting a chair in her path—but wisely retaining a grip on it.

She threw back her head and laughed, loudly, insultingly. Her broad hands, now gloveless and as red as broiled lobsters, found resting-places on her hips. He allowed his gaze to take them in with one hurried, sweeping glance. They were as big and as menacing as a prizefighter's.

"We'll discuss it when you're sober," he made haste to say, trying to wink amiably.

"So help me Mike, I haven't touched a—" she began, but caught herself in time. "So yez discharge me, do yez?" she shouted.

"I understood you had quit, anyway."

"Well, me fine little man, I'll see yez further before I'll quit now. I came back this minute to give notice, but I wouldn't do it now for twenty-five dollars."

13

"You don't have to give notice. You're discharged. Good-bye." He started for the sitting-room.

She slapped the dining-table with one of her big hands. The dishes bounced into the air, and so did he.

"I'll give this much notice to yez," she roared, "and ye'll bear it in mind as long as yez stay in the same house wid me. I don't take no orders from the likes of you. I was employed by Miss Duluth. I cook for her, I get me pay from her, and I'll not be fired by anybody but her. Do yez get that? I'd as soon take orders from the kid as from you, ye little pinhead. Who are yez anyhow? Ye're nobody. Begorry, I don't even know yer name. Discharge me! Phy, phy, ye couldn't discharge a firecracker. What's that?"

"I—I didn't say anything," he gasped.

"Ye'd better not."

"I shall speak to—to Miss Duluth about this," he muttered, very red in the face.

"Do!" she advised, sarcastically. "She'll tell yez to mind yer own business, the same as I do. The idee! Talkin' about firing me! Fer the love av Mike, Annie, what do yez think av the nerve? Phy Miss Duluth kapes him on the place I can't fer the life av me see. She's that tinder-hearted she—"

But he had bolted through the door, slamming it after him. As he reached the bottom of the stairs leading to his bedroom the door opened again and Annie called out to him:—

"Are you through lunch, sir?"

He was halfway up the steps before he could frame an answer. Tears of rage and humiliation were in his baby-blue eyes.

"Tell her to go to the devil," he sputtered.

As he disappeared at the bend in the stairs he distinctly heard Annie say:—

"I can see myself doing it—not."

For an hour he paced the floor of his little bed-chamber, fuming and swearing to himself in a mild, impotent fashion—and in some dread of the door. Such words and sentences as these fell from his lips:—"Nobody!" "Keeps me on the place!" "Because she's tender-hearted!" "I will fire her!" "Can't talk back to me!" "Damned Irisher!" And so on and so forth until he quite wore himself out. Then he sat down at the window and let the far-away look slip back into his troubled blue eyes. They began to smart, but he did not blink them.

Phoebe found him there at four when she came in for her nap. He promised to play croquet with her.

Dinner was served promptly that evening, and it was the best dinner Bridget had cooked in a month.

"That little talk of mine did some good," said he to himself, as he selected a toothpick and went in to read "Nicholas Nickleby" till bedtime. "They can't fool with me."

He was reading Dickens. His wife had given him a complete set for Christmas. To keep him occupied, she said.

CHAPTER II

MISS NELLIE DULUTH

Nellie Duluth had an apartment up near the Park, the upper end of the Park, in fact, and to the east of it. She went up there, she said, so that she could be as near as possible to her husband and daughter. Besides, she hated taking the train at the Grand Central on Sundays. She always went to One Hundred and Twenty-fifth Street in her electric brougham. It didn't seem so far to Tarrytown from One Hundred and Twenty-fifth. In making her calculations Nellie always went through the process of subtracting forty-two from one-twenty-five, seldom correctly. She had no difficulty in taking the two from the five, but it wasn't so simple when it came to taking four from two with one to carry over. It was the one that confused her. For the life of her she couldn't see what became of it. Figures of that sort were not in her line.

Nellie's career had been meteoric. She literally had leaped from the chorus into the rôle of principal comédienne—one of those pranks of fortune that cannot be explained or denied. She was one of the "Jack-in-the-Box" girls in a big New York production. On the opening night, when the lid of her box flew open and she was projected into plain view, she lost her bearings and missed the tiny platform in coming down. To save herself from an ignominious tumble almost to the footlights she hopped off the edge of her box, where she had been "teetering" helplessly, and did a brief but exceedingly graceful little "toe spin," hopping back into the box an instant later with all the agility of a scared rabbit. She expected "notice" from the stage manager for her inexcusable slip.

But the spectators liked it. They thought it was in the play. She was so pretty, so sprightly, so graceful, and so astoundingly modest that they wanted more of her. After the performance no fewer than a dozen men asked the producer why he didn't give that little girl with the black hair more of a chance.

The next night she was commanded to repeat the trick. Then they permitted her to do it over in the "encore." Before the end of a fortnight she was doing a dance with the comedian, exchanging lines with him. Then a little individual song-and-dance specialty was introduced. At the close of the engagement on Broadway she announced that she would not sign for the next season unless given a "ripping" part and the promise to be featured.

That was three years ago. Now she was the feature in the big, musical comedy success, "Up in the Air" and had New York at her feet. The critics admitted that she saved the "piece" in spite of composer and librettist. Some one is always doing that very thing for the poor wretches, Heaven pity them.

Nellie was not only pretty and sprightly, but as clever as they make them. She never drew the short straw. She had a brain that was quite as active as her feet. It was not a very big brain; for that matter, her feet were tiny. She had the good sense to realise that her brain would last longer than her feet, so she got as much for them as she could while the applause lasted. She drove shrewd bargains with the managers and shrewder ones with Wall Street admirers, who experienced a slim sense of gratification in being able to give her tips on the market, with the assurance that they would see to it that she didn't lose.

She put her money into diamonds as fast as she got it. Some one in the profession had told her that diamonds were safer than banks or railroad bonds. She could get her interest by looking at them and she could always sell them for what she paid for them.

The card on the door of her cosey apartment bore the name, "Miss Nellie Duluth."

There was absolutely nothing inside or outside the flat to lead one to suspect that there was a Mr. Duluth. A husband was the remotest figure in her household. When the management concluded to put her name in the play-bill, after the memorable Jack-in-the-Box leap, she was requested to drop her married name, because it would not look well in print.

"Where were you born?" the manager had asked.

"Duluth."

"Take Duluth for luck," said he, and Duluth it was. She changed the baptismal name Ella to Nellie. At home in Blakeville she had been called Eller or Ell.

Her apartment was an attractive one. Her housemaid was a treasure. She was English and her name was Rachel. Nellie's personal maid and dresser was French. Her name was Rebecca. When Miss Duluth and Rebecca left the apartment to go to the theatre in the former's electric brougham, Rachel put the place in order. So enormous was the task that she barely had it finished when her mistress returned, tired and sleepy, to litter it all up again with petticoats, stockings, roses, orchids, lobster shells, and cigarette stubs. More often than otherwise Nellie brought home girls from the theatre to spend the night with her. Poor things, they were chorus girls, just as she had been, and they had so far to go. Besides, they served as excuses for declining unwelcome invitations to supper. Be that as it may, Rachel had to clean up after them, finding their puffs, rats, and switches in the morning and the telephone number at their lodgings in the middle of the night. She had her instructions to say that such young ladies were spending the night with Miss Duluth.

"If you don't believe it, call up Miss Duluth's number in the telephone book," she always concluded, as if the statement needed verification.

Nellie had not been in Tarrytown for a matter of three weeks; what with rehearsals, revisions, consultations, and suppers, she just couldn't get around to it. The next day after Harvey's inglorious stand before Bridget she received a letter from him setting forth the whole affair in a peculiarly vivid light. He said that something would have to be done about Bridget and advised her to come out on the earliest day possible to talk it over with him. He confessed to a hesitancy about discharging the cook, recalling the trouble she had experienced in getting her away from a neighbour in the first place. But Bridget was drinking and quarrelling with Annie and using strong language in the presence of Phoebe. He would have discharged her long ago if it hadn't been for the fear of worrying her during rehearsals and all that. She wasn't to be bothered with trifling household squabbles at such an important time as this. No, sir! Not if he could help it. But, just the same, he thought she'd better come out and talk it over before Bridget took it into her head to poison some one.

"I really, truly must go up to Tarrytown next Sunday," said Nellie to the select company supping in her apartment after the performance that night. "Harvey's going to discharge the cook."

"Who is Harvey?" inquired the big blond man who sat beside her.

"My teenty-weenty hubby," said she, airily.

There were two other men besides the big blond in the party, and the wife of one of them—a balance wheel.

The big blond man stared at his hostess. He expected her to laugh at her own joke, but she did not. The others were discussing the relative merits of the Packard and Peerless cars. He waited a moment and then leaned closer to Nellie's ear.

"Are you in earnest?" he asked, in low tones.

"About what, Mr. Fairfax?"

"Hubby. Have you got one?"

"Of course I have. Had him for six years. Why?"

He swallowed hard. A wave of red crept up over his jowl and to the very roots of his hair.

18

"I've known you for over a month, Nellie," he said, a hard light in his fishy grey eyes, "and you've never mentioned this husband of yours. What's the game?"

"It's a guessing game," she said, coolly. "You might guess what I'm wearing this little plain gold ring on my left hand for. It's there where everybody can see it, isn't it? You just didn't take the trouble to look, Mr. Fairfax. Women don't wear wedding rings for a joke, let me tell you that."

"I never noticed it," he said, huskily. "The truth is, it never entered my head to think you could be a married woman."

"Thought I was divorced, eh?"

"Well, divorces are not uncommon, you know. You girls seem to get rid of husbands quite as easily as you pick them up."

"Lord bless you," said Nellie, in no way offended, "I have never done anything to give Harvey cause for divorce, and I'm sure he's never done the tiniest thing out of the way. He never treats me cruelly, he never beats me, he doesn't get tight and break things up, and he never looks at other women. He's the nicest little husband ever."

She instructed Rachel to fill up Mr. Fairfax's glass and pass the ripe olives. He was watching her, an odd expression in his eyes. A big, smooth-faced man of fifty was he, fat from high living, self-indulgence, and indolence, immaculately dressed to the tips of his toes.

"Speaking of divorce," she went on, without looking at him, "your wife didn't have much trouble getting hers, I've heard."

It was a daring thing to say, but Nellie was from the West, where courage and freshness of vision are regarded as the antithesis of tact and diplomacy. Tact calls for tact. The diplomatist is powerless if you begin shooting at him. Nellie did not work this out for herself; she merely wanted to put him in a corner where he would have to stand and get it over with.

Fairfax was disconcerted. He showed it. No one ever presumed to discuss the matter with him. It was a very tender subject. His eyes wavered.

"I like your cheek," he growled.

"Don't you like to talk about it?" she inquired, innocently.

"No," he replied, curtly. "It's nobody's business, Miss Duluth."

"My, how touchy!" She shivered prettily. "I feel as if some one had thrown a pail of ice water over me."

"We were speaking of your—this husband of yours," he said, quietly. "Why have you never mentioned him to me? Is it quite fair?"

"It just slipped my mind," she said, in the most casual way. "Besides, I thought you knew. My little girl is four—or is it five?"

"Where do you keep them?"

"I've got 'em in storage up at Tarrytown. That's the Sleepy Hollow neighbourhood, isn't it? I guess that's why Harvey likes it so well."

"What is his business?"

She looked up quickly. "What is that to you, Mr. Fairfax?"

"Nothing. I am in no way interested in Mr. Duluth."

"His name isn't Duluth," she flashed, hotly. "If you are not interested in him, let's drop the subject."

"I retract what I said. I am always interested in curiosities. What's he like?"

"Well, he's like a gentleman, if you are really interested in curiosities," she said.

He laughed. "By Jove, you've got a ready wit, my dear." He looked at her reflectively, speculatively. "It's rather a facer to have you turn out to be a married woman."

"Don't you like married women?"

"Some of 'em," he answered, coolly. "But I don't like to think of you as married."

"Pooh!" she said, and there was a world of meaning in the way she said it.

"Don't you know that it means a great deal to me?" he demanded, leaning closer and speaking in a lowered voice, tense and eager.

"Pooh!" she repeated.

He flushed again. "I cannot bear the thought of you belonging—"

She interrupted him quickly. "I wouldn't say it, if I were you."

"But I must say it. I'm in love with you, Nellie, and you know it. Every drop of blood in my veins is crying out for you, and has been—"

Her face had clouded. "I've asked you not to say such things to me."

He stared in amazement. "You are dreaming! I've never uttered a word of this sort to you. What are you thinking of? This is the first time I've said—"

Nellie was dismayed. It was the first time he had spoken to her in that way. She stammered something about "general principles," but he was regarding her so fixedly that her attempt at dissembling was most unconvincing.

"Or perhaps," said he, almost savagely, but guardedly, "you are confusing me with some one else."

This was broad enough to demand instant resentment. She took refuge in the opportunity.

"Do you mean to insult me, Mr. Fairfax?" she demanded, coldly, drawing back in her chair.

He laughed harshly.

"Is there any one else?" he asked, gripping one of her small hands in his great fist.

She jerked the hand away. "I don't like that, Mr. Fairfax. Please remember it. Don't ever do it again. You have no right to ask such questions of me, either."

"I'm a fool to have asked," he said, gruffly. "You'd be a fool to answer. We'll let it go at that. So that's your wedding ring, eh? Odd that I shouldn't have noticed it before."

She was angry with herself, so she vented the displeasure on him.

"You never took much notice of your wife's wedding ring, if tales are true."

"Please, Miss Duluth, I—"

"Oh, I read all about the case," she ran on. "You must have hated the notoriety. I suppose most of the things she charged you with were lies."

He pulled his collar away from his throat.

"Is it too hot in the room?" she inquired, innocently.

His grin was a sickly one. "Do you always make it so hot?" he asked. "This is my first visit to your little paradise, you must remember. Don't make it too hot for me."

"It isn't paradise when it gets too hot," was her safe comment.

Fairfax's wife had divorced him a year or two before. The referee was not long in deciding the case in her favour. As they were leaving Chambers, Fairfax's lawyer had said to his client:—"Well, we've saved everything but honour." And Fairfax had replied:—"You would have saved that, too, if I had given you a free rein." From which it may be inferred that Fairfax was something of a man despite his lawyer.

He was one of those typical New Yorkers who were Pittsburgers or Kansas Citians in the last incarnation—which dated back eight or ten years, at the most, and which doesn't make any difference on Broadway—with more money than he was used to and a measureless capacity for spending. His wife had married him when money was an object to him. When he got all the money he wanted he went to New York and began a process of elevating the theatre by lending his presence to the stage door. The stage declined to be elevated without the aid of an automobile, so he also lent that, and went soaring. His wife further elevated the stage by getting a divorce from him.

"This is my first time here," he went on, "but it isn't to be the last, I hope. What good taste you have, Nellie! It's a corking little nest."

"I just can't go out to Tarrytown every night," she explained. "I must have a place in town."

"By the way," he said, more at ease than he had been, "you spoke of going to Tarrytown on Sunday. Let me take you out in the motor. I'd like to see this husband chap of yours and the little girl, if—"

"Nay, nay," she said, shaking her head. "I never mix my public affairs with my private ones. You are a public affair, if there ever was one. No, little Nellie will go out on the choo-choos." She laughed suddenly, as if struck by a funny thought. Then, very seriously, she said:—"I don't know what Harvey would do to you if he caught you with me."

He stiffened. "Jealous, eh?"

"Wildly!"

"A fire-eater?"

"He's a perfect devil," said Nellie, with the straightest face imaginable.

Fairfax smiled in a superior sort of way, flecked the ashes from his cigarette, and leaned back in his chair the better to contemplate the charming creature at his side. He thoroughly approved of jealous husbands. The fellow who isn't jealous, he argued, is the hardest to trifle with.

"I suppose you adore him," he said, with a thinly veiled sneer.

"'He's the idol of me 'art,'" she sang, in gentle mimicry.

"Lucky dog," he whispered, leering upon her. "And how trustful he is, leaving you here in town to face temptation alone while he hibernates in Tarrytown."

"He trusts me," she flashed.

"I am the original 'trust buster,'" he laughed.

Nellie arose abruptly. She stretched her arms and yawned. The trio opposite gave over disputing about automobiles, and both men looked at their watches.

22

"Go home," said Nellie. "I'm tired. We've got a rehearsal to-morrow."

No one took offence. They understood her ways.

Fairfax gave her his light topcoat to hold while he slipped into it. She was vaguely surprised that he did not seek to employ the old trick of slipping an arm about her during the act. Somehow she felt a little bit more of respect for him.

"Don't forget to-morrow night," he said, softly, at the door. "Just the four of us, you know. I'll come back for you after the play."

"Remember, it has to be in the main restaurant," she warned him. "I like to see the people."

He smiled. "Just as you like."

She laughed to herself while Rebecca was preparing her for bed, tickled by the thought of the "fire-eating" Harvey. In bed, however, with the lights out, she found that sleep would not come as readily as she had expected. Instead her mind was vividly awake and full of reflections. She was thinking of the two in Tarrytown asleep for hours and snugly complacent. Her thoughts suddenly leaped back to the old days in Blakeville when she was the Town Marshal's daughter and he the all-important dispenser of soft drinks at Davis'. How she had hung on his every word, quip, or jest! How she had looked forward to the nights when he was to call! How she hated the other girls who divided with her the attentions of this popular young beau! And how different everything was now in these days of affluence and adulation! She caught herself counting how many days it had been since she had seen her husband, the one-time hero of her dreams. What a home-body he was! What a change there was in him! In the old Blakeville days he was the liveliest chap in town. He was never passive for more than a minute at a stretch. Going, gadding, frivolling, flirting—that was the old Harvey. And now look at him!

Those old days were far, far away, so far that she was amazed that she was able to recall them. She had sung in the church choir and at all of the local entertainments. The praise of the Blakeville *Patriot* was as sweet incense to her, the placid applause of the mothers' meetings more riotous than anything she could imagine in these days when audiences stamped and clapped and whistled till people in the streets outside the theatre stopped and envied those who were inside.

And then the days of actual courtship; she tried to recall how and when they began. She married Harvey in the little church on the hill. Everybody in town was there. She could close her eyes now and see Harvey in the new checked suit he had ordered from Chicago especially for the occasion, a splendid innovation that caused more than one Lotharial eye to gleam with envy.

Then came the awakening. The popular drug clerk, for all his show of prosperity and progress, had not saved a cent in all his years of labour, nor was there any likelihood of his salary ever being large enough to supply the wants of two persons. They went to live with his mother, and it was not long before he was wearing the checked suit for "everyday use" as well as for Sunday.

She was stagestruck. For that matter, so was he. They were members of the town dramatic club and always had important parts in the plays. An instructor came from Chicago to drill the "members of the cast," as they were designated by the committee in charge. It was this instructor who advised Nellie to go to Chicago for a course in the school he represented. He assured her she would have no difficulty in getting on the stage.

Harvey procured a position in a confectioner's establishment in State Street and she went to work for a photographer, taking her lessons in dancing, singing, and elocution at odd hours. She was pretty, graceful, possessed of a lovely figure not above the medium height; dark-haired and vivacious after a fashion of her own. As her pleased husband used to say, she "got a job on the stage before you could say Jack Robinson." He tried to get into the chorus with her, but the management said, "No husbands need apply."

That was the beginning of her stage career, such a few years ago that she was amazed when she counted back. It seemed like ten years, not five.

She soared; he dropped, and, as there was no occasion for rousing himself, according to the point of view established by both of them, he settled back into his natural groove and never got beyond his soda-fountain days in retrospect.

The next night after the little supper at Nellie's a most astonishing thing happened. A smallish man with baby-blue eyes appeared at the box-office window, gave his name, and asked for a couple of good seats in Miss Duluth's name. The ticket-seller had him repeat the name and then gruffly told him to see the company manager.

"I'm Miss Duluth's husband," said the smallish man, shrinking. The tall, flashily good-looking man at his elbow straightened up and looked at him with a doubtful expression in his eyes. He was Mr. Butler, Harvey's next-door neighbour in Tarrytown. "You must be new here."

"Been here two years," said the ticket-seller, glaring at him. "See the manager."

"Where is he?"

"At his hotel, I suppose. Please move up. You're holding the line back."

At that moment the company's press representative sauntered by. Nellie's husband, very red in the face and humiliated, hailed him, and in three minutes was being conducted to a seat in the nineteenth row, three removed from the aisle, followed by his Tarrytown neighbour, on whose face there was a frozen look of disgust.

"We'll go back after the second act," said Harvey, struggling with his hat, which wouldn't go in the rack sideways. "I'll arrange everything then."

"Rotten seats," said Mr. Butler, who had expected the front row or a box.

"The scenery is always better from the back of the house," explained his host, uncomfortably.

"Damn the scenery!" said Mr. Butler. "I never look at it."

"Wait till you see the setting in the second—" began Harvey, with forced enthusiasm, when the lights went down and the curtain was whisked upward, revealing a score of pretty girls representing merry peasants, in costumes that cost a hundred dollars apiece, and glittering with diamond rings.

Mr. Butler glowered through the act. He couldn't see a thing, he swore.

"I should think the husband of the star could get the best seats in the house," he said when the act was half-over, showing where his thoughts were.

"That press agent hates me," said Harvey, showing where his had been.

"Hates you? In God's name, why?"

"I've had to call him down a couple of times," said Harvey, confidentially. "Good and hard, too."

"I suppose that's why he makes you take a back seat," said Butler, sarcastically.

"Well, what can a fellow do?" complained the other. "If I could have seen Mr. —"

A man sitting behind tapped him on the shoulder.

"Will you be good enough to stop talking while the curtain's up?" he requested, in a state of subdued belligerency.

Harvey subsided without even so much as a glance to see what the fellow was like.

After the act Butler suggested a drink, which was declined.

"I don't drink," explained Harvey.

His companion snorted. "I'd like to know what kind of a supper we're going to have if you don't drink. Be a sport!"

"Oh, don't you worry about that," said Harvey. "Ginger ale livens me up as much as anything. I used to simply pour the liquor down me. I had to give it up. It was getting the best of me. You should have seen the way I was carrying on out there in Blakeville before—"

"Well, come out and watch me take a drink," interrupted Butler, wearily. "It may brace you up."

Harvey looked helplessly at the three ladies over whom they would have to climb in order to reach the aisle and shook his head.

"We're going out after the next act. Let's wait till then."

"Give me my seat check," said Butler, shortly. "I'm going out." Receiving the check, he trampled his way out, leaving Harvey to ruminate alone.

The joint presence of these two gentlemen of Tarrytown in the city requires an explanation. You may remember that Nellie's husband resented Butler's habit of ignoring him. Well, there had come a time when Butler had thought it advisable to get down from his high horse. His wife had gone to Cleveland to visit her mother for a week or two. It was a capital time for him to get better acquainted with Miss Duluth, to whom he had been in the habit of merely doffing his hat in passing.

The morning of his wife's departure, which was no more than eight hours prior to their appearance at the box office, he made it a point to hail Harvey in a most jovial manner as he stood on his side porch, suggesting that he come over and see the playroom he had fixed up for his children and Phoebe.

"We ought to be more neighbourly," he said, as he shook hands with Harvey at the steps. Later on, as they smoked in the library, he mentioned the fact that he had not had the pleasure of seeing Miss Duluth in the new piece.

Harvey was exalted. When any one was so friendly as all this to him he quite lost his head in the clouds.

"We'll go in and see it together," said he, "and have a bit of supper afterward."

"That's very good of you," said Butler, who was gaining his point.

"When does Mrs. Butler return?" asked Harvey.

Butler was startled. "Week or ten days."

"Well, just as soon as she's back we'll have a little family party—"

His neighbour shook his head. "My wife's in mourning," he said, nervously.

"In mourning?" said Harvey, who remembered her best in rainbow colours.

"Yes. Her father."

"Dead?"

"Certainly," said Butler, a trifle bewildered. He coughed and changed the current of conversation. It was not at all necessary to say that his wife's father had been dead eleven years. "I thought something of going in to the theatre to-night," he went on. "Just to kill time. It will be very lonely for me, now that my dear wife's away."

Harvey fell into the trap. "By jinks!" he exclaimed, "what's the matter with me going in, too? I haven't been in town at night for six weeks or more."

Butler's black eyes gleamed.

"Excellent! We'll see a good play, have a bite to eat, and no one will know what gay dogs we are." He laughed and slapped Harvey on the back.

"I'll get seats for Nellie's show if you'd like to see it," said Harvey, just as enthusiastically, except that he slapped the arm of the chair and peeled his knuckle on a knob he hadn't seen.

"Great!"

"And say, I'd like you to know my wife better, Mr. Butler. If you don't object I'll ask her to go out with us after the show for something to eat."

"Permit me to remind you, Mr.—Mr.—er—"

"Call me Harvey," said the owner of the name.

"—to remind you that this is my party. I will play host and be honoured if your wife will condescend to join me—and you—at any hour and place she chooses."

"You are most kind," said Harvey, who had been mentally calculating the three one-dollar bills in his pocket.

And that is how they came to be in the theatre that night.

The curtain was up when Butler returned. He had had a drink.

"Did you send a note back to your wife?" he asked as he sat down.

"What for?"

"To tell her we are here," hissed the other.

"No, I didn't," said Harvey, calmly. "I want to surprise her."

Butler said something under his breath and was so mad during the remainder of the act that everybody on the stage seemed to be dressed in red.

Miss Duluth did not have to make a change of costume between the second and third acts. It was then that she received visitors in her dressing-room. She had a sandwich and a glass of milk at that time, but was perfectly willing to send across the alley for bottled beer if her callers cared to take anything so commonplace as that.

She was sitting in her room, quite alone, with her feet cocked upon a trunk, nibbling a sandwich and thinking of the supper Fairfax was to give later on in the evening, when the manager of the company came tapping at her door. People had got in the habit of walking in upon her so unexpectedly that she issued an order for every one to knock and then made the injunction secure by slipping the bolt. Rebecca went to the door.

"Mr. Fairfax is here, mademoiselle," she announced a moment later. "Mr. Ripton has brought him back and he wants to come in." Except for the word "mademoiselle" Rebecca spoke perfect English.

Nellie took one foot down and then, thinking quickly, put it up again. It wouldn't hurt Fairfax, she argued, to encounter a little opposition.

"Tell Ripton I'm expecting some one else," she said, at random. "If Mr. Fairfax wants to wait in the wings, I'll see him there."

But she had not the slightest inkling of what was in store for her in the shape of visitors.

At that very moment Harvey and his friend were at the stage door, the former engaged in an attempt at familiarity with the smileless attendant.

"Hello, Bob; how goes it?" said he, strutting up to the door.

Bob's bulk blocked the passage.

"Who d'you want to see?" he demanded, gruffly.

"Who d'you suppose?" asked Harvey, gaily.

"Don't get fresh," snapped the door man, making as if to slam the iron door in his face. Suddenly he recognised the applicant. "Oh, it's you, is it?"

"You must be going blind, Bobby," said Harvey, in a fine effort at geniality. "I'm taking a friend in to show him how it's done. My friend, Mr. Butler, Bob."

Mr. Butler stepped on Harvey's toes and said something under his breath.

"Is Miss Duluth expecting you, Mr.—er—Mr.—Is she?" asked old Bob.

"No. I'm going to surprise her."

Bob looked over his shoulder hastily.

"If I was you," he said, "I'd send my card in. She's—she's nervous and a shock might upset her."

"She hasn't got a nerve in her body," said Harvey. "Come on, Butler. Mind you don't fall over the braces or get hit by the scenery."

They climbed a couple of steps and were in the midst of a small, bustling army of scene shifters and property men. Old Bob scratched his head and muttered something about "surprises."

Three times Harvey tried to lead the way across the stage. Each time they were turned back by perspiring, evil-minded stage hands who rushed at them with towering, toppling canvases. Once Harvey nearly sat down when an unobserving hand jerked a strip of carpet from under his feet. A grand staircase almost crushed Mr. Butler on its way into place, and some one who seemed to be in authority shouted to him as he dodged:—

"Don't knock that pe-des-tal over, you pie face!"

At last they got safely over, and Harvey boldly walked up to the star's dressing-room.

"We're all right now," he said to Butler, with a perceptible quaver in his voice. "Just you wait while I go in and tell her I am here."

Butler squeezed himself into a narrow place, where he seemed safe from death, mopped his brow, and looked like a lost soul.

Two men, sitting off to the left, saw Harvey try the locked door and then pound rather imperatively.

"Good Lord!" exclaimed one of them, staring. "It's—it's—er—What's-His-Name, Nellie's husband! Well, of all the infernal—"

"That?" gasped Fairfax.

"What in thunder is he doing here this time o' night! Great Scott, he'll spoil everything," groaned Ripton, the manager.

Harvey pounded again with no response. Nellie was sitting inside, mentally picturing the eagerness that caused Fairfax to come a-pounding like that. She had decided not to answer.

Ripton called a stage hand.

"Tell him that Nellie isn't seeing anybody to-night," he whispered. "Do it quick. Get him out of here."

"Shall I throw him out, sir?" demanded the man, with a wry face. "Poor little chap!"

"Just tell him that Nellie will see him for a few minutes after the play." Then, as the man moved away:—"They've got no business having husbands, Mr. Fairfax. Damned nuisances."

Fairfax had his hand to his lips. He was thinking of Nellie's "perfect devil."

"I fancy he doesn't cut much of a figure in her life," said he, in a tone of relief.

In the meantime the stage hand had accosted Harvey, who had been joined by the anxious Mr. Butler.

"Miss Duluth ain't seeing any one to-night, sir," he said. "She gave strict orders. No one, sir."

Harvey's blue eyes were like delft saucers. "She'll see me," he said. "I'm her husband, you know."

"I know that, sir. But the order goes, just the same."

"Is she ill?"

"Yes, sir. Very ill," said the man, quickly.

Butler was gnawing his moustache.

"Rubbish!" he said, sharply. "Come away, you. She's got a visitor in there. Can't you see the lay of the land?"

The little husband turned cold, then hot.

"A—a man visitor?"

"Certainly," snapped the aggrieved Mr. Butler. "What else?"

Without another word, Harvey brushed past the stage hand and began rattling the door violently.

"Nellie!" he shouted, his lips close to the paint.

In a second the door flew open and the astonished actress stood there staring at him as if he were a ghost. He pushed the door wide open and strode into the dressing-room, Nellie falling back before him. The room was empty save for the dismayed Rebecca.

"There!" he exclaimed, turning to address Butler in the doorway, but Butler was not there. The stage hand had got in his way.

"Wha—what, in the name of Heaven, are you doing here, Harvey?" gasped Nellie.

"How are you, Nell? Nothing serious, I hope."

"Serious?" she murmured, swallowing hard, her wits in the wind.

"Ain't you ill?"

"Never was better in my life," she cried, seeing what she thought was light. "Who brought you to town with such a tale as that? I'm fine. You've been fooled. If I were you, I'd take the first train out and try to find out who—"

"It's all right, Butler," he called out. "Come right in. Hello! Where are you?" He stepped to the door and looked out. Mr. Butler was being conducted toward the stage door by the burly stage hand. He was trying to expostulate. "Hi! What you doing?" shouted Harvey, darting after them. "Let my friend alone!"

Up came Ripton in haste.

"O'Brien, what do you mean? Take your hand off that gentleman's shoulder at once. He is a friend of Mr.—Mr.—ahem! A terrible mistake, sir."

Then followed a moment of explanation, apology, and introduction, after which Harvey fairly dragged his exasperated friend back to Nellie's room.

She was still standing in the middle of the room trying to collect her wits.

"You remember Mr. Butler, deary," panted Harvey, waving his hand. Nellie gasped in the affirmative.

At that instant Fairfax's big frame appeared in the door. He was grinning amiably. She glared at him helplessly for a moment.

"Won't you introduce me to your husband?" he said, suavely.

Nellie found her tongue and the little man shook hands with the big one.

"Glad to meet you," said Harvey.

"I am glad to see you," said Fairfax, warmly.

31

"My friend Butler," introduced Harvey.

Mr. Butler was standing very stiff and pallid, with one knee propped against a chair. There was a glaze over his eyes. Fairfax grinned broadly.

"Oh, Butler and I are old acquaintances," said he. "Wife out of town, Butler?"

"Sure," said Harvey, before Butler could reply. "And we're in town to see the sights. Eh, Butler?"

Butler muttered something that sounded uncommonly like "confounded ass," and began fanning himself with his derby hat and gloves and walking-stick, all of which happened to be in the same hand.

"We're going to take Nellie—I mean Miss Duluth—out for supper after the play," went on Harvey, glibly. "We'll be waiting for you, dearie. Mr. Butler is doing the honours. By the way, Butler, I think it would be nicer if Nellie could suggest an odd lady for us. We ought to have four. Do you know of any one, Nell? By George, we've got to have a pretty one, though. We insist on that, eh, Butler?" He jabbed Butler in the ribs and winked.

"Don't do that!" said the unhappy Mr. Butler, dropping his stick. It rolled under a table and he seized the opportunity thus providentially presented. He went down after it and was lost to view for a considerable length, of time, hiding himself as the ostrich does when it buries its head in the sand and imagines it is completely out of sight.

Nellie's wits were returning. She was obliged to do some rapid and clever thinking. Fairfax was watching her with a sardonic smile on his lips. Ripton, the manager, peered over his shoulder and winked violently.

"Oh, Harvey dear," she cried, plaintively, "how disappointed I am. I have had strict orders from the doctor to go straight home to bed after every performance. I really can't go with you and Mr. Butler to-night. I wish you had .gn +1 telephoned or something. I could have told you."

Harvey looked distressed. "What does the doctor say it is?"

Fairfax was sitting on a trunk, a satisfied smile on his lips

"My heart," she said, solemnly.

"Don't you think you could go out for a—just a sandwich and a bottle of beer?" he pleaded, feeling that he had wantonly betrayed his friendly neighbour.

"Couldn't think of it," she said. "The nurse will be here at eleven. I'll just have to go home. He insists on absolute quiet for me and I'm on a dreadful diet." A bright thought struck her. "Do you know, I have to keep my door locked so as not to be startled by—"

The sharp, insistent voice of the callboy broke in on her flow of excuses.

"There! I'll have to go on in a second. The curtain's going up. Good-night, gentlemen. Good-night, Harvey dear. Give me a kiss."

She pecked at his cheek with her carmine lips.

"Just half an hour at some quiet little restaurant," he was saying when she fled past him toward the stage.

"Sorry, dear," she called, then stopped to speak to Mr. Butler. "Thank you so much, Mr. Butler. Won't you repeat the invitation some time later on? So good of you to bring Harvey in. Bring Mrs. Butler in some night, and if I'm better we will have a jolly little spree, just the four of us. Will you do it?"

She beamed on him. Butler bowed very low and said:—

"It will give me great pleasure, Miss Duluth."

"Good-night, then."

"Good-night."

When she returned to her dressing-room later on, she found Fairfax there, sitting on a trunk, a satisfied smile on his lips. She left the door open.

Mr. Ripton conducted the two men across to the stage door, leading them through the narrow space back of the big drop. Chorus girls threw kisses at Harvey; they all knew him. He winked blandly at Butler, who was staring straight before him.

"A great life, eh?" said Harvey, meaning that which surrounded them. They were in the alley outside the stage door.

"I'm going to catch the ten-twenty," said Butler, jamming his hat down firmly.

"Ain't you going to see the last act?" demanded the other, dismayed.

Butler lifted his right hand to heaven, and, shaking it the better to express the intensity of his declaration, remarked:—

"I hope somebody will kick me all over town if I'm ever caught being such a damned fool as this again. I honestly hope it! I've been made ridiculous—a blithering fool! Why, you—you—" He paused in his rage, a sudden wave of pity assailing him. "By George, I can't help feeling sorry for you! Good-night."

Harvey hurried after him.

"I guess I'll take it, too. That gets us out at eleven-thirty. We can get a bite to eat in the station, I guess."

He had to almost trot to keep pace with Butler crossing to the Grand Central. Seated side by side in the train, and after he had recovered his breath a bit, he said:—

"Confound it, I forgot to ask Nellie if it will be wise for her to come out on Sunday. The heart's a mighty bad thing, Butler."

"It certainly is," said Butler, with unction.

At the station in Tarrytown he said "Good-night" very gruffly and hurried off to jump into the only cab at the platform. He had heard all about Blakeville and the wild life Harvey had led there, and he was mad enough to fight.

"Good-night, Mr. Butler," said Harvey, as the hack drove off.

He walked up the hill.

CHAPTER III

MR. FAIRFAX

He found the nursemaid up and waiting for him. Phoebe had a "dreadful throat" and a high temperature. It had come on very suddenly, it seems, and if Annie's memory served her right it was just the way diphtheria began. The little girl had been thrashing about in the bed and whimpering for "daddy" since eight o'clock. His heart sank like lead, to a far deeper level than it had dropped with the base desertion of Butler. Filled with remorse, he ran upstairs without taking off his hat or overcoat. The feeling of resentment toward Butler was lost in this new, overpowering sense of dread; the discovery of his own lamentable unfitness for "high life" expeditions faded into nothingness in the face of this possible catastrophe. What if Phoebe were to die? He would be to blame. He remembered feeling that he should not have left her that evening. It had been a premonition, and this was to be the price of his folly.

At three in the morning he went over to rouse the doctor, all the time thinking that, even if he were capable of forgiving himself for Phoebe's death, Nellie would always hold him responsible. The doctor refused to come before eight o'clock, and slammed the door in the disturber's face.

"If she dies," he said to himself over and over again as he trudged homeward, "I'll kill that beast of a doctor. I'll tear his heart out."

The doctor did not come till nine-thirty. They never do. He at once said it was a bad attack of tonsilitis, and began treatment on the stomach. He took a culture and said he would let Mr.—Mr. What's-His-Name know whether there was anything diphtheritic. In the meantime, "Take good care of her."

Saturday morning a loving note came from Nellie, deploring the fact that she couldn't come out on Sunday after all. The doctor said she must save her strength. She instructed Harvey to dismiss Bridget and get another cook at once. But Harvey's heart had melted toward Bridget. The big Irishwoman was the soul of kindness now that her employer was in distress.

About nine o'clock that morning a man came up and tacked a placard on the door and informed the household that it was in quarantine. Harvey went out and looked at the card. Then he slunk back into Phoebe's room and sat down, very white and scared.

"Do you think she'll die?" he asked of the doctor when that gentleman called soon afterward. He was shivering like a leaf.

"Not necessarily," said the man of medicine, calmly. "Diphtheria isn't what it used to be."

"If she dies I'll jump in the river," said the little father, bleakly.

"Nonsense!" said the doctor. "Can you swim?" he added, whimsically.

"No," said Harvey, his face lighting up.

The doctor patted him on the back. "Brace up, sir. Has the child a mother?"

Harvey stared at him. "Of course," he said. "Don't you know whose child you are 'tending?"

"I confess I—er—I—"

"She is the daughter of Nellie Duluth."

"Oh!" fell from the doctor's lips. "And you—you are Miss Duluth's husband? I didn't quite connect the names."

"Well, I'm her husband, name or no name," explained the other. "I suppose I ought to send for her. She ought to know."

"Are you—er—separated?"

"Not at all," said Harvey. "I maintain two establishments, that's all. One here, one in the city."

"Oh, I see," said the doctor, who didn't in the least see. "Of course, she would be subject to quarantine rules if she came here, Mr.—Mr.—ahem!"

"They couldn't get along without her at the theatre," groaned the husband.

"I'd suggest waiting a day or two. Believe me, my dear sir, the child will pull through. I will do all that can be done, sir. Rest easy." His manner was quite different, now that he knew the importance of his patient. He readjusted his glasses and cleared his throat. "I hope to have the pleasure of seeing Mrs.—er —your wife, sir."

"She has a regular physician in town," said Harvey, politely.

For two weeks he nursed Phoebe, day and night, announcing to the doctor in the beginning that his early training made him quite capable. There were moments when he thought she was dying, but they passed so quickly that his faith in the physician's assurances rose above his fears. Acting on the purely unselfish motive that Nellie would be upset by the news, he kept the truth from her, and she went on singing and dancing without so much as a word to distress her. Two Sundays passed; her own lamentable illness kept her away from the little house in Tarrytown.

"If we tell her about Phoebe," said Harvey to Bridget and Annie, "she'll go all to pieces. Her heart may stop, like as not. Besides, she'd insist on coming out and taking care of her, and that would be fatal to the show. She's never had diphtheria. She'd be sure to catch it. It goes very hard with grown people."

"Have you ever had it, sir?" asked Annie, anxiously.

"Three times," said Harvey, who hadn't thought of it up to that moment.

When the child was able to sit up he put in his time reading "David Copperfield" to her.

Later on he played "jacks" with her and cut pictures out of the comic supplements. By the end of the month he was thinner and more "peaked," if anything, than she. Unshaven, unshorn, unpressed was he, but he was too full of joy to give heed to his own personal comforts or requirements.

His mind was beginning to be sorely troubled over one thing. Now that Phoebe was well and getting strong he realised that Nellie would be furious when she found out how ill the child had been and how she had been deceived. He considered the advisability of keeping it from her altogether, swearing every one to secrecy, but there was the doctor's bill to be paid. When it came to paying that Nellie would demand an explanation. It was utterly impossible for him to pay it himself. Thinking over his unhappy position, he declared, with a great amount of zeal, but no vigour, that he was going to get a job and be independent once more. More than that, when he got fairly well established in his position (he rather leaned toward the drug or the restaurant business) he would insist on Nellie giving up her arduous stage work and settling down to enjoy a life of comfort and ease—even luxury, if things went as he meant them to go.

One afternoon late in October, when the scarlet leaves were blowing across his little front yard and the screens had been taken from the windows, a big green automobile stopped at his gate and a tall man got out and came briskly up the walk. Harvey was sitting in the library helping Phoebe with her ABC's when he caught sight of the visitor crossing the porch.

"Gentleman to see you," said Annie, a moment later.

"Is it the butcher's man? I declare, I must get in and attend to that little account. Tell him I'll be in, Annie."

"It ain't the butcher. It's a swell."

Harvey got up, felt of the four days' growth of beard on his chin, and pondered.

"Did he give his name?"

"Mr. Fairfax, he said."

He remembered Fairfax. His hand ran over his chin once more.

"Tell him to come in. I'll be down in fifteen minutes."

He went upstairs on the jump and got his razor out. He was nervous. Only that morning he had written to Nellie telling her of Phoebe's expensive illness and of her joyous recovery. The doctor's bill was ninety dollars. He cut himself in three places.

Fairfax was sitting near the window talking with Phoebe when he clattered downstairs ten minutes later, deploring the cuts but pleased with himself for having broken all records at shaving. The big New Yorker had a way with him; he could interest children as well as their mothers and grown sisters. Phoebe was telling him about "Jack the Giant Killer" when her father popped into the room.

"Phoebe!" he cried, stopping short in horror.

Fairfax arose languidly.

"How do you do, Mr.—ah—ahem! The little girl has been playing hostess. The fifteen minutes have flown."

"Ten minutes by my watch," said Harvey, promptly. "Phoebe, dear, where did you get that awful dress—and, oh, my! those dirty hands? Where's Annie? Annie's the nurse, Mr. Fairfax. Run right away and tell her to change that dress and wash your hands. How do you do, Mr. Fairfax? Glad to see you. How are you?"

He advanced to shake the big man's hand. Fairfax towered over him.

"I was afraid you would not remember me," said Fairfax.

"Run along, Phoebe. She's been very ill, you see. We don't make life any harder for her than we have to. Washing gets on a child's nerves, don't you think? It used to on mine, I know. Of course I remember you. Won't you sit down? Annie! Oh, Annie!"

He called into the stair hallway and Annie appeared from the dining-room.

"Ann—Oh, here you are! How many times must I tell you to put a clean dress on Phoebe every day? What are her dresses for, I'd like to know?" He winked violently at Annie from the security of the portière, which he held at arm's length as a shield. Annie arose to the occasion and winked back.

"May I put on my Sunday dress?" cried Phoebe, gleefully.

"Only one of 'em," said he, in haste. "Annie will pick out one for you."

Considerably bewildered, Phoebe was led away by the nurse.

"She's a pretty child," said Fairfax. If his manner was a trifle strained Harvey failed to make note of it. "Looks like her mother."

"I'm glad you think so," said the father, radiantly. "I'd hate to have her look like me."

Fairfax looked him over and suppressed a smile.

"She is quite happy here with you, I suppose," he said, taking a chair.

"Yes, sir-ree."

"Does she never long to be with her mother?"

"Well, you see," said Harvey, apologising for Nellie, "she doesn't see much of Miss—of her mother these days. I guess she's got kind of used to being with me. Kids are funny things, you know."

"She seems to have all the comforts and necessities of life," said the big man, looking about him with an affectation of approval.

"Everything that I can afford, sir," said Harvey, blandly.

"Have you ever thought of putting her in a nice school for—"

"She enters kindergarten before the holidays," interrupted the father.

"I mean a—er—sort of boarding school," put in the big man, uneasily. "Where she could be brought up under proper influences, polished up, so to speak. You know what I mean. Miss Duluth has often spoken of such an arrangement. In fact, her heart seems to be set on it."

"You mean she—she wants to send her away to school?" asked Harvey, blankly.

"It is a very common and excellent practice nowadays," said the other, lamely.

The little man was staring at him, his blue eyes full of dismay.

"Why—why, I don't believe I'd like that," he said, grasping the arms of his chair with tense fingers. "She's doing all right here. It's healthy here, and I am sure the schools are good enough. Nellie has never said anything to me about boarding school. Why—why, Mr. Fairfax, Phoebe's only five—not quite that, and I—I think it would be cruel to put her off among strangers. When she's fifteen or sixteen, maybe, but not now. Nellie don't mean that, I'm sure."

"There is a splendid school for little girls up in Montreal—a sort of convent, you know. They get the best of training, moral, spiritual, and physical. It is an ideal life for a child. Nellie has been thinking a great deal of sending her there. In fact, she has practically decided to—"

Harvey came to his feet slowly, dizzily.

"I can't believe it. She wouldn't send the poor little thing up there all alone; no, sir! I—I wouldn't let her do it." He was pacing the floor. His forehead was moist.

"Miss Duluth appreciates one condition that you don't seem able to grasp," said Fairfax, bluntly. "She wants to keep the child as far removed from stage life and its environments as possible. She wants her to have every advantage, every opportunity to grow up entirely out of reach of the—er—influences which now threaten to surround her."

Harvey stopped in front of him. "Is this what you came out here for, Mr. Fairfax? Did Nellie tell you to do this?"

"I will be perfectly frank with you. She asked me to come out and talk it over with you."

"Why didn't she come herself?"

"She evidently was afraid that you would overrule her in the matter."

"I never overruled her in my life," cried Harvey. "She isn't afraid of me. There's something else."

"I can only say, sir, that she intends to put the child in the convent before Christmas. She goes on the road after the holidays," said Fairfax, setting his huge jaw.

Harvey sat down suddenly, limp as a rag. His mouth filled with water—a cold, sickening moisture that rendered him speechless for a moment. He swallowed painfully. His eyes swept the little room as if in search of something to prove that this was the place for Phoebe—this quiet, happy little cottage of theirs.

"Before Christmas?" he murmured.

"See here, Mr.—ah—Mr., here is the situation in a nutshell:—Nellie doesn't see why she should be keeping up two establishments. It's expensive. The child will be comfortable and happy in the convent and this house will be off her hands. She—"

"Why don't she give up her flat in town?" demanded Harvey, miserably. "That's where the money goes."

"She expects to give it up the first of the year," said Fairfax. "The road tour lasts till May. She is going to Europe for the summer."

"To Europe?" gasped Harvey, feeling the floor sink under his feet.

He did not think to inquire what was to become of him in the new arrangement.

"She needs a sea voyage, travel—a long vacation, in fact. It is fully decided. So, you see, the convent is the place for Phoebe."

"But where do I come in?" cried the unhappy father. "Does she think for a minute that I will put my child in a convent so that we may be free to go to Europe and do things like that? No, sir! Dammit, I won't go to Europe and leave Phoebe in a—"

Fairfax was getting tired of the argument. Moreover, he was uncomfortable and decidedly impatient to have it over with. He cut in rather harshly on the other's lamentations.

"If you think she's going to take you to Europe, you're very much mistaken. Why, man, have you no pride? Can't you understand what a damned useless bit of dead weight you are, hanging to her neck?"

It was out at last. Harvey sat there staring at him, very still; such a pathetic figure that it seemed like rank cowardice to strike again. And yet Fairfax, now that he had begun, was eager to go on striking this helpless, inoffensive creature with all the frenzy of the brutal victor who stamps out the life of his vanquished foe.

"She supports you. You haven't earned a dollar in four years. I have it from her, and from others. It is commonly understood that you won't work, you won't do a stroke toward supporting the child. You are a leech, a barnacle, a —a—well, a loafer. If you had a drop of real man's blood in you, you'd get out and earn enough to buy clothes for yourself, at least, and the money for a hair cut or a shoe shine. She has been too good to you, my little man. You can't blame her for getting tired of it. The great wonder is that she has stood for it so long."

Words struggled from Harvey's pallid lips.

"But she loves me," he said. "It's all understood between us. I gave her the start in life. She will tell you so. I—"

"You never did a thing for her in your life," broke in the big man, harshly. He was consumed by an ungovernable hatred for this little man who was the husband of the woman he coveted.

"I've always wanted to get a job. She wouldn't let me," protested Harvey, a red spot coming into each of his cheeks. "I don't want to take the money she earns. I never have wanted to. But she says my place is here at home, with

Phoebe. Somebody's got to look after the child. We've talked it over a—"

"I don't want to hear about it," snapped Fairfax, hitting the arm of his chair with his fist. "You're no good, that's all there is to it. You are a joke, a laughing stock. Do you suppose that she can possibly love a man like you? A woman wants a man about her, not the caricature of one."

"I intend to get a job as soon as—" began Harvey, as if he had not heard a word his visitor was saying.

"Now, see here," exclaimed Fairfax, coming to his feet. "I'm a man of few words. I came out here to make you a proposition. It is between you and me, and no one need be the wiser. I'm not such a fool as to intrust a thing of this kind to an outsider. Is there any likelihood of any one hearing us?"

Nellie's husband shrank lower into his chair and shook his head. He seemed to have lost the power of speech. Fairfax drew a chair up closer, however, and lowered his voice.

"You've got a price. Men of your type always have. I told Nellie I would see you to-day. I'll be plain with you. She's tired of you, of this miserable attachment. You are impossible. That's settled. We won't go into that. Now I'm here, man to man, to find out how much you will take and agree to a separation."

Harvey stiffened. He thought for a moment that his heart had stopped beating.

"I don't believe I understand," he muttered.

"Don't you understand the word 'separation'?"

"Agree to a separation from what? Great God, you don't mean a separation from Phoebe?"

"Don't be a fool! Use your brain, if you've got one."

"Do—you—mean—Nellie?" fell slowly, painfully from the dry lips of the little man in the Morris chair.

"Certainly."

"Does she want to—to leave me?" The tears started in his big blue eyes. He blinked violently.

"It has come to that. She can't go on as she has been going. It's ridiculous. You are anxious to go back to Blakeville, she says. Well, that's where you belong. Somebody's drug store out there you'd like to own, I believe. Now, I am prepared to see that you get that drug store and a matter of ten or twenty thousand dollars besides. Money means nothing to me. All you have to do is to make no answer to the charges she will bring—"

43

Harvey leaped to his feet with a cry of abject pain.

"Did she send you here to say this to me?" he cried, shrilly, his figure shaking with suppressed fury.

"No," said Fairfax, involuntarily drawing back. "This is between you and me. She doesn't know—"

"Then, damn you!" shrieked Harvey, shaking his fist in the big man's face, "what do you mean by coming here like this? What do you think I am? Get out of here! I'm a joke, am I? Well, I'll show you and her and everybody else that I'm a hell of a joke, let me tell you that! I was good enough for her once. I won her away from every fellow in Blakeville. I can do it again. I'll show you, you big bluffer! Now, get out! Don't you ever come here again, and— don't you ever go near my wife again!"

Fairfax had arisen. He was smiling, despite his astonishment.

"I fancy you will find you can't go so far as that," he sneered.

"Get out, or I'll throw you out!"

"Better think it over. Twenty-five thousand and no questions asked. Take a day or two to think—"

With a shriek of rage Harvey threw himself at the big man, striking out with all his might. Taken by surprise, Fairfax fell away before the attack, which, though seemingly impotent, was as fierce as that of a wildcat.

The New Yorker was in no danger. He warded off the blows with ease, all the time imploring the infuriated Harvey to be sensible, to be calm. But with a heroism born of shame and despair the little man swung his arms like windmills, clawing, scratching, until the air seemed full of them. Fairfax's huge head was out of reach. In his blind fury Harvey did not take that into account. He struck at it with all the power in his thin little arms, always falling so far short that the efforts were ludicrous.

Fairfax began to look about in alarm. The noise of the conflict was sure to attract the attention of the servants. He began backing toward the doorway. Suddenly Harvey changed his fruitless tactics. He drove the toe of his shoe squarely against the shinbone of the big man. With a roar of rage Fairfax hurled himself upon the panting foe.

"I'll smash your head, you little devil," he roared, and struck out viciously with one of his huge fists.

The blow landed squarely on Harvey's eye. He fell in a heap several feet away. Half-dazed, he tried to get to his feet. The big man, all the brute in him aroused, sprang forward and drove another savage blow into the bleak, white face of the little one. Again he struck. Then he lifted Harvey bodily from the floor and held him up against the wall, his big hand on his throat.

"How do you like it?" he snarled, slapping the helpless, half-conscious man in the face with his open hand—loud, stinging blows that almost knocked the head off the shoulders. "Will you agree to my proposition now?"

From Harvey's broken lips oozed a strangled—

"No!"

Fairfax struck again and then let him slide to the floor.

"You damned little coward!" he grated. "To kick a man like that!"

He rushed from the room, grabbed his hat and coat in the hall, and was out of the house like a whirlwind.

The whir of a motor came vaguely, indistinctly to Harvey's ears. He was lying close to the window. As if in a dream he lifted himself feebly to his knees and looked out of the window, not knowing exactly what he did nor why he did it.

A big green car was leaving his front gate. He was a long time in recalling who came up in it.

His breath was coming slowly. He tried to speak, but a strange, unnatural wheeze came from his lips. A fit of coughing followed. At last he got upon his feet, steadying himself against the window casing. For a long time he stood there, working it all out in his dizzy, thumping brain.

He put his hand to his lips and then stared dully at the stains that covered it when he took it away. Then it all came back to him with a rush. Like a guilty, hunted thing he slunk upstairs to his room, carefully avoiding the room in which Phoebe was being bedecked in her Sunday frock. Her high, shrill voice came to his ears. He was weeping bitterly, sobbing like a whipped child.

He almost fainted when he first peered into the mirror on his bureau. His eyes were beginning to puff out like great knobs, his face and shirt front were saturated with his own plucky blood. Plucky! The word occurred to him as he looked. Yes, he had been plucky. He didn't know it was in him to be so plucky. A sort of pride in himself arose to offset the pain and mortification. Yes, he had defended his honour and Nellie's. She should hear of it! He would tell her what he had done and how Fairfax had struck him down with a chair. She would then deny to him that she had said those awful things about him. She would be proud of him!

Carefully he washed his hands and face. With trembling fingers he applied court-plaster to his lips, acting with speed because his eyes were closing. Some one had told him that raw beefsteak was good for black eyes. He

45

wondered if bacon would do as well. There was no beefsteak in the house.

His legs faltered as he made his way to the back stairs. Bridget was coming up. She started back with a howl.

"Come here, Bridget," he whispered. "Into my room. Be quick!" He retreated. He would employ her aid and swear her to secrecy. The Irish know a great deal about fighting, he reflected.

"In the name av Hivvin, sor, what has happened to yez?" whispered Bridget, aghast in the doorway.

"Come in and I'll tell you," said he, with a groan.

Presently a childish voice came clamouring at the locked door. He heard it as from afar. Bridget paused in her ministrations. He had just said:—

"I will take boxing lessons and physical culture of your brother, Bridget. You think he can build me up? I know I'm a bit run down. No exercise, you know. Still, I believe I would have thrashed him to a frazzle if I hadn't stumbled. That was when he kicked me here. I got this falling against the table."

"Yis, sor," said Bridget, dutifully.

In response to the pounding on the door, he called out, bravely:—

"You can't come in now, Phoebe. Papa has hurt himself a little bit. I'll come out soon."

"I got my Sunday dress on, daddy," cried the childish voice. "And I'm all spruced up. Has the nice gentleman gone away?"

His head sank into his hands.

"Yes, dearie, he's gone," he replied, in muffled tones.

46

CHAPTER IV

LUNCHEON

For several days, he moped about the house, not even venturing upon the porch, his face a sight to behold. His spirits were lower than they had been in all his life. The unmerciful beating he had sustained at the hands of Fairfax was not the sole cause of his depression. As the consequences of that pummelling subsided, the conditions which led up to it forced themselves upon him with such horrifying immensity that he fairly staggered under them.

It slowly dawned on him that there was something very sinister in Fairfax's visit, something terrible. Nellie's protracted stay in town, her strange neglect of Phoebe, to say nothing of himself, the presence of Fairfax in her dressing-room that night, and a great many circumstances which came plainly to mind, now that he considered them worth while noticing, all went a long way toward justifying Fairfax in coming to him with the base proposition that had resulted so seriously to his countenance.

Nellie was tired of him! He did not belong to her world. That was the sum and substance of it. As he dropped out of her world, some one else quite naturally rose to fill the void. That person was Fairfax. The big man had said that she wanted a separation, she wanted to provide a safe haven for Phoebe. The inference was plain. She wanted to get rid of him in order to marry Fairfax. Fairfax had been honest enough to confess that he was acting on his own initiative in proposing the bribe, but there must have been something behind it all.

He had spoken of "charges." What charge could Nellie bring against him? He was two days in arriving at the only one—failure to provide. Yes, that was it. "Failure to provide." How he hated the words. How he despised men who did not provide for their wives. He had never thought of himself in that light before. But it was true, all true. And Nellie was slipping away from him as the result. Not only Nellie but Phoebe. She would be taken from him.

"I don't drink," he argued with himself, "and I've never treated her cruelly. Other women don't interest me. I never swear at her. I've never beaten her. I've always loved her. So it must be that I'm 'no good,' just as that scoundrel says. 'No good!' Why, she knows better than that. There never was a fellow who worked harder than I did for Mr. Davis. I drew trade to his store. Anybody in Blakeville will swear to that. Haven't I tried my best to get a job in the same shows with her? Wasn't I the best comedian they had in the

47

dramatic club? I've never had the chance to show what I could do, and Nellie knows it. But I'll show them all! I'll make that big brute wish he'd never been born. I'll—I'll assert myself. He shan't take her away from me."

His resolutions soared to great heights, only to succumb to chilly blasts that sent them shrivelled back to the lowest depths. What could he do against a man who had all the money that Fairfax possessed? What could he offer for Nellie, now that some one else had put a stupendous price on her? He remembered reading about an oil painting that originally sold for five hundred francs and afterward brought forty thousand dollars. Somehow he likened Nellie to a picture, with the reservation that he didn't believe any painting on earth was worth forty thousand dollars. If there was such a thing, he had never seen it.

Then he began to think of poor Nellie cast helpless among the tempters. She was like a child among voracious beasts of prey. No wonder she felt hard toward him! He was to blame, terribly to blame. In the highest, most exalted state of remorse he wept, not once but often. His poor little Nellie!

In one of these strange ever-growing flights of combined self-reproach and self-exaltation he so vividly imagined himself as a rescuer, as an able-bodied defender against all the ills and evils that beset her, that the fancy took the shape of positive determination. He made up his mind to take her off the stage, back to Blakeville, and to an environment so sweet and pure that her life would be one long season of joy and happiness.

With the growth of this resolution he began to plan his own personal rehabilitation. First of all, he would let his face recover its natural shape; then he would cultivate muscle and brawn at the emporium of Professor Flaherty; moreover, he would devote considerable attention to his own personal appearance and to the habits of the "men about town." He would fight the tempters with their own weapons—the corkscrew, the lobster pick, the knife and fork, and the nut-splitter!

He did not emerge from the house for five days. By that time he was fairly presentable.

It was Annie's day out, so he took Phoebe for a little walk. As for Phoebe, she never passed a certain door upstairs without kicking at it with first one, then the other of her tiny feet, in revenge for the way it had hurt her father by remaining open so that he could bump into it on that bloody, terrifying day. She sent little darts of exquisite pain through him by constantly alluding to the real devastator as "that nice Mr. Fairy-fax." It was her pleasure to regard him as a great big fairy who had promised her in secret that she would some day be like Cinderella and have all the riches the slipper showered upon that poor little lady.

As they were returning home after a stroll through a rather remote street, they came upon Mr. Butler, who was down on his knees fixing something or other about his automobile. Harvey thought it a good opportunity to start his crusade against New York City.

"Hello," he said, halting. Butler looked up. He was mad as a wet hen to begin with.

"Hello," he snarled, resuming his work.

"I've been thinking about that little—"

"Get out of the light, will you?"

Harvey moved over, dragging Phoebe after him.

"That little scheme of ours to dine together in town some night. You remember we talked about it—"

"No, I don't," snapped Butler.

"We might lunch together early next week. I know a nice little place on Seventh Avenue where you get fine spaghetti. We—"

"I'm booked for a whole month of luncheons," said Butler, sitting back on his heels to stare at this impossible person. "Can't join you."

"Some other time, then," said Harvey, waving his hand genially. "Your wife home yet?"

Butler got upon his feet.

"Say," said he, aggressively, "do you know she's heard about that idiotic trip of mine to town that night? Fairfax told everybody, and somebody's wife told Mrs. Butler. It got me in a devil of a mess."

"You don't say so!"

"Yes, I do say so. Next time you catch me—But, what's the use?" He turned to his work with an expressive shrug of his shoulders.

"I'll have my wife explain everything to Mrs. Butler the first time she comes out," said Harvey, more bravely than he felt. He could not help wondering when Nellie would come out.

"It isn't necessary," Butler made haste to assure him.

Harvey was silent for a moment.

"Fixing your automobile?" he asked, unwilling to give it up without another effort.

"What do you suppose I'm doing?"

"It's wonderful how fast one of these little one-seated cars can go," mused Harvey. "Cheap, too; ain't they?"

Butler faced him again, malice in his glance.

"It's not in it with that big green car your wife uses," he said, distinctly.

"Big green—" began Harvey, blankly. Then he understood. He swallowed hard, straightened Phoebe's hat with infinite care and gentleness, and looking over Butler's head, managed to say, quite calmly:—"It used to be blue. We've had it painted. Come along, Phoebe, Mr. Butler's busy. We mustn't bother him. So long, Butler."

"So long," said Mr. Butler, suddenly intent upon finding something in the tool-box.

The pair moved on. Out of the corner of his eye Butler watched them turn the corner below.

"Poor little guy!" he said to the monkey wrench.

The big green car! All the way home that juggernaut green car ran through, over, and around him. He could see nothing else, think of nothing else. A big green car!

That evening he got from Bridget the address of her brother, Professor Flaherty, the physical trainer and body builder.

In the morning he examined himself in the mirror, a fever of restlessness and impatience afflicting him with the desire to be once more presentable to the world. He had been encouraged by the fact that Butler had offered no comment on the black rims around his eyes. They must be disappearing.

With his chin in his hands he sat across the room staring at his reflection in the glass, a gloomy, desolate figure.

"It wouldn't be wise to apply for a job until these eyes are all right again," he was saying to himself, bitterly. "Nobody would hire a man with a pair of black eyes and a busted lip—especially a druggist. I'll simply have to wait a few days longer. Heigh-ho! To-morrow's Sunday again. I—I wonder if Nellie will be out to see us."

But Nellie did not come out. She journeyed far and fast in a big green car, but it was in another direction.

Thursday of the next week witnessed the sallying forth of Harvey What's-His-

Name, moved to energy by a long dormant and mournfully acquired ambition. The delay had been irksome.

Nellie's check for the month's expenses had arrived in the mail that morning. He folded it carefully and put it away in his pocketbook, firmly resolved not to present it at the bank. He intended to return it to her with the announcement that he had secured a position and hereafter would do the providing.

Spick and span in his best checked suit, his hat tilted airily over one ear, he stepped briskly down the street. You wouldn't have known him, I am sure, with his walking-stick in one hand, his light spring overcoat over the other arm. A freshly cleaned pair of grey gloves, smelling of gasoline, covered his hands. On the lapel of his coat loomed a splendid yellow chrysanthemum. Regular football weather, he had said.

The first drug store he came to he entered with an air of confidence. No, the proprietor said, he didn't need an assistant. He went on to the next. The same polite answer, with the additional information, in response to a suggestion by the applicant, that the soda-water season was over. Undaunted, he stopped in at the restaurant in the block below. The proprietor of the place looked so sullen and forbidding that Harvey lost his courage and instead of asking outright for a position as manager he asked for a cup of coffee and a couple of fried eggs. As the result of this extra and quite superfluous breakfast he applied for the job.

The man looked him over scornfully.

"I'm the manager and the whole works combined," he said. "I need a dish-washer, come to think of it. Four a week and board. You can go to work to-day if—"

But Harvey stalked out, swinging his cane manfully.

"Well, God knows I've tried hard enough," he said to himself, resignedly, as he headed for the railway station. It was still six minutes of train time. "I'll write to Mr. Davis out in Blakeville this evening. He told me that my place would always be open to me."

It was nearly one o'clock when he appeared at Nellie's apartment. Rachel admitted him. He hung his hat and coat on the rack, deposited his cane in the corner, and sauntered coolly into the little sitting-room, the maid looking on in no little wonder and uneasiness.

"Where's my wife?" he asked, taking up the morning paper from the centre table and preparing to make himself at home in the big armchair.

"She's out to lunch, sir."

51

He laid the paper down.

"Where?"

Rachel mentioned a prominent downtown café affected by the profession.

"Will you have lunch here, sir?" she inquired.

"No," said he, determinedly. "Thank you just the same. I'm lunching downtown. I—I thought perhaps she'd like to join me."

Rachel rang for the elevator and he departed, amiably doffing his hat to her as he dropped to the floor below.

At one of the popular corner tables in the big café a party of men and women were seated, seven or eight in all. Nellie Duluth had her back toward the other tables in the room. It was a bit of modesty that she always affected. She did not like being stared at. Besides, she could hold her audience to the very end, so to speak, for all in the place knew she was there and were willing to wait until she condescended to face them in the process of departure.

It was a very gay party, comprising a grand-opera soprano and a tenor of world-wide reputation, as well as three or four very well-known New Yorkers. Manifestly, it was Fairfax's luncheon. The crowd at this table was observed by all the neck-craners in the place. Every one was telling everyone else what every one knew:—"That's Nellie Duluth over there."

As the place began to clear out and tables were being abandoned here and there, a small man in a checked suit appeared in the doorway. An attendant took his hat and coat away from him while he was gazing with kaleidoscopic instability of vision upon the gay scene before him. He had left his walking-stick in a street car, a circumstance which delayed him a long time, for, on missing it, he waited at a corner in the hope of recognising the motorman on his return trip up Madison Avenue.

The head-waiter was bowing before him and murmuring, "How many, sir?"

"How many what?" mumbled Harvey, with a start.

"In your party?" asked the man, not half so politely and with a degree of distance in his attitude. It did not look profitable.

"Oh! Only one, sir. Just a sandwich and a cup of coffee, I think."

There was a little table away over in the corner sandwiched between the doors of entrance and egress for laden waiters and 'bus boys. Toward this a hastily summoned second or third assistant conducted the newcomer. Twice during the process of traversing this illimitable space Harvey bumped against chairs occupied by merry persons who suddenly became crabbed and asked him who the devil he was stumbling over.

A blonde, flushed woman who sat opposite Nellie at the table in the corner caught sight of him as he passed. She stared hard for a moment and then allowed a queer expression to come into her eyes.

"For Heaven's sake!" she exclaimed, with considerable force.

"What's the matter? Your husband?" demanded Nellie Duluth, with a laugh.

"No," she said, staring harder. "Why, I can't be mistaken. Yes, as I live, it's Mr.—Mr. What's-His-Name, your husband, Nellie."

"Don't turn 'round, Nellie," whispered Fairfax, who sat beside her.

"I don't believe it!" cried Nellie, readily. "It isn't possible for Harvey to be here. Where is he?" she demanded in the same breath, looking over her shoulder.

Harvey was getting out of the way of a 'bus boy and a stack of chinaware and in the way of a waiter with a tray of peach Melbas when she espied him.

"For the land's sake!" she gasped, going clear back to Blakeville for the expression. "I don't dare look, Carrie. Tell me, has he got a—a fairy with him? Break it gently."

"Fairy?" sneered Fairfax, suddenly uncomfortable. "Why, he's lost in the wood. He's alone on a desert isle. What the deuce is he doing here?"

Harvey gave his order to the disdainful waiter and then settled back in his chair for the first deliberate look around the room in quest of his wife.

Their eyes met. She had turned halfway round in her chair and was looking at him with wide-open, unbelieving eyes. He felt himself suddenly tied hand and foot to the chair. Now that he had found her he could do no more than stare at her in utter bewilderment. He had come tilting at windmills.

The flush deepened in her cheek as she turned her attention to the dessert that had just been set down before her. She was very quiet, in marked contrast to her mood of the moment before.

Fairfax made a remark which set the others to laughing. She did not smile, but toyed nervously with the dessert fork. Under cover of the laughter he leaned over and whispered, an anxious, troubled note in his voice:—

"I'll call the head waiter and have him put out before he does anything crazy."

"Put out?" she repeated. "Why, what do you think he'd try to do?"

"He's got an ugly look in his eye. I tell you, he'll create a scene. That's what he's here for. You remember what happened—"

She laughed shrilly. "He won't shoot any one," she said in his ear. "Harvey create a scene! Oh, that's rich!"

"He hasn't forgotten the thrashing I gave him. He has been brooding over it, Nellie." Fairfax was livid about the eyes.

"Well, I respect him for trying to thrash you, even though he got the worst of it." She looked again in Harvey's direction. He was still staring steadily at her. "He's all alone over there and he's miserable. I can't stand it. I'm going over to sit with him."

As she arose Fairfax reached out and grasped her arm.

"Don't be a fool," he said, in dismay.

"I won't," she replied, sweetly. "Trust me. So long, people. I'm going over to have coffee with my husband."

If the occupants of the big café were surprised to see Nellie Duluth make her way over to the table and sit down with the queer little person in checks, not so Harvey. He arose to greet her and would have kissed her if she had not restrained him. He was gratified, overjoyed, but not surprised.

"Hello!" she said, sharply, to cover the inward disquiet that possessed her. She was looking intently into his eyes as if searching for something she dreaded.

"Hello!" was his response. He was still a trifle dazed.

She sat down opposite him. Before she could think of anything further to say the head waiter rushed up to inquire if Miss Duluth and her friend wouldn't prefer a table at one of the windows.

"No, this will do," she said, thankful for the interruption.

"We are doing very nicely," said Harvey, rather pompously, adding in a loud voice of authority:—"Tell that fellow to hustle my luncheon along, will you?" Then, turning to Nellie, he said:—"You don't look as though you'd ever been sick a day in your life, Nellie."

She laughed uncomfortably. "How are you, Harvey? And Phoebe?"

"Fine. Never better. Why don't you come out and see us occasionally?"

"May I order a cup of black coffee?" she asked, ignoring the question. She was sorely puzzled.

"Have a big one," he urged, signalling a waiter.

Her curiosity conquered. "What in Heaven's name brought you here, Harvey?"

He told her of the word Rachel had given him. Nellie made a mental note of the intention to speak plainly to Rachel.

"Who are your friends?" he asked. Just then he caught a glimpse of Fairfax's face. He turned very cold.

"Mr. Fairfax is giving a luncheon for two of the grand-opera people," she explained.

He forced his courage. "I don't want you to have anything more to do with that man," he said. "He's a scoundrel."

"Now, don't be silly," she cried. "What train are you going out on?"

"I don't know. Maybe I'll stay in. I'll go up to your flat, I guess, for a couple of days. Phoebe's all right. She's over the diphtheria now—"

"Diphtheria?" gasped Nellie, wide-eyed, overlooking his other declaration, which, by the way, was of small moment.

"Almost died, poor kiddie."

She flared up in an instant. "Why wasn't I told? What were you thinking of, you little fool?"

"If you had taken the trouble to come out to Tarrytown, you could have found out for yourself," he retorted, coolly. "Now, see here, Nellie, I've come in to see you and to have a very plain talk with you. So just hold your horses. Don't fly off the handle. I am the head of this family and I'm going to boss it from this time on."

"You—" she began, in a furious little shriek, her eyes blazing. She caught herself up in time. Two or three people nearby looked up at the sound of her raised voice. She lowered it to a shrill, intense half-whisper. "What do you mean by coming here in this way? Everybody is laughing at me. You make me ridiculous. I won't stand for it; do you hear?"

He was colder if possible than before, but he was resolute.

"We've got to have an understanding, the sooner the better," he said, quietly.

"Yes, you're right," she repeated; "the sooner the better."

"We can't talk here," he said, suddenly conscious that the eyes of many were upon them. "Go over and ask that infernal sneak to excuse you, and we'll go up to the flat."

"I'm going motoring this aft—"

"You do as I tell you!" said he, in a strange voice.

"Why, Harvey—" she stammered, catching her breath.

"When you've had your coffee," he added.

She sipped her coffee in silence, in wonder, in bitter resentment. He munched the club sandwich and sucked the coffee through his thin moustache with a vehemence that grated on her nerves terribly.

"I've had all I want," she said, suddenly putting the little cup down with a crash.

"Then go over and tell 'em you've got to go home."

She crossed the room, red-faced and angry. He watched her as she made an announcement to the party, saw them laugh uproariously, and smiled in triumph over the evidence of annoyance on the part of Fairfax. Nellie was whispering something close to the big man's ear, and he was shaking his head vigorously. Then she waved her hand to the party and started away. Fairfax arose to follow her. As he did so, Harvey came to his feet and advanced. The big man stopped short, with a look of actual alarm in his eyes, and went back to his seat, hastily motioning to the head waiter.

Five minutes later Miss Duluth emerged from the café, followed by the little man in the checked suit.

An attendant blew his whistle and called out down the line of waiting motors: —

"Mr. Fairfax's car up!"

"Get me a taxi," ordered Nellie, hastily.

The man betrayed his surprise. She was obliged to repeat the order.

"What does a taxi to—to our place cost?" demanded Harvey, feeling in his pocket.

"Never mind," she snapped. "I'll pay for it."

"No, you won't," he asserted. "I raised seventeen dollars yesterday on the watch mother gave me. It's my own money, Nellie, remember that."

Rachel was plainly amazed when the couple walked into the apartment. The two at once resumed the conversation they had carried on so vigorously in the taxicab on the way up from downtown. Nellie did not remove her hat, sharply commanding Rachel to leave the room.

"No," she said, "she simply has to go to the convent. She'll be safe there, no matter how things turn out for you and me, Harve, I insist on that."

"Things are going to turn out all right for us, Nellie," he protested, a plaintive

56

note in his voice. It was easily to be seen which had been the dominating force in the ride home.

"Now, you've got to be reasonable, Harve," she said, firmly. "We can't go on as we have been going. Something's just got to happen."

"Well, doggone it, haven't I said that I'll agree to your trip to Europe? I won't put a stop to that. I see your point clearly. The managers think it wise for you to do a bit of studying abroad. I can see that. I'm not going to be mean. Three months' hard work over there will get you into grand-opera sure. But that has nothing to do with Phoebe. She can go to Blakeville with me, and then when you come back next fall I'll have a job here in New York and we'll—"

"Don't talk foolishness," she blurted out. "You've said that three or four times. First you wanted me to go back to Blakeville to live. You insisted on it. What do you think I am? Why, I wouldn't go back to Blakeville if Heaven was suddenly discovered to be located there instead of up in the sky. That's settled. No Blakeville for me. Or Phoebe either. Do you suppose I'm going to have that child grow up like—like"—she changed the word and continued —"like a yap?"

"All I ask is that you will give me a chance to show what I can do," he said, earnestly.

"You can do that just as well with Phoebe in the convent, as I've said before."

"She's as much my child as she is yours," he proclaimed, stoutly.

"Then you ought to be willing to do the sensible thing by her."

"Why, good Lord, Nell, she's only five," he groaned. "She'll die of homesickness."

"Nonsense! She'll forget both of us in a month and be happy."

"She won't forget me!" he exclaimed.

"Well, I've said my say," she announced, pacing the floor. "Suppose we agree to disagree. Well, isn't it better to have her out of the mess?"

"I won't give her up, derned if I do!"

"Say, don't you know if it comes to a question of law, the Court will give her to me?"

"I'm not trying to take her away from you."

"You're trying to ruin my career."

"Fairfax has put all this into your head, Nellie, dear. He's a low-down rascal."

"He's my friend, and a good one, too. I don't believe he offered you that money to agree to a separation."

"Darn it all, you can still see the scar on my lip. That ought to prove something. If I hadn't stumbled, I'd have knocked him silly. As it was, he kicked me in the face when I was down."

"He told me you assaulted him without cause."

"He lied."

"Well, that's neither here nor there. I'm sorry you were beaten up so badly. It wasn't right, I'll admit. He said you were plucky, Harve. I couldn't believe him at first."

His face brightened.

"You give me a chance and I'll show you how plucky I am!" he cried. "Come on now, Nellie, let's make a fresh start."

She was silent for a long time. At heart she was fair and honest. She had lost her love and respect for the little man, but, after all, was that altogether his fault? She was sorry for him.

"Well, I'll think it over," she said, at last.

"I'll write to Mr. Davis to-night!" he cried, encouraged.

"All right. I hope he'll give you a job," said she, also brightening, but for an entirely different reason.

"You'll give up this awful thing of—of separating; won't you?"

"I'll promise one thing, Harvey," said she, suddenly sincere. "I won't do anything until I come back from the road. That's fair, isn't it? And I'll tell you what else I'll do. I will let Phoebe stay with you in Tarrytown until the end of the tour—in May."

"But I'm going to Blakeville," he protested.

"No," said she, firmly, "I won't agree to that. Either you stay in Tarrytown or she goes to the convent."

"I can't get work in Tarrytown."

"You can tell Mr. Davis you will come out to Blakeville in time for the opening of the soda-water season. I'll do the work for the family till then. That's all I'll consent to. I'll ask for a legal separation if you don't agree to that."

"I—I'll think it over," he said, feebly; "I'll stay here with you for a couple of days, and—"

"You will do nothing of the sort!" she cried. "Do you suppose I'm going to spoil my chances for a separation, if I want to apply, by letting you live in the same house with me? Why, that would be wasting the two months already gone."

He did not comprehend, and he was afraid to ask for an explanation. The term "failure to provide" was the only one he could get through his head; "desertion" was out of the question. His brow was wet with the sweat of a losing conflict. He saw that he would have to accept her ultimatum and trust to luck to provide a way out of the difficulty. Time would justify him, he was confident. In the meantime, he would ease his conscience by returning the check, knowing full well that it would not be accepted. He would then take it, of course, with reservations. Every dollar was to be paid back when he obtained a satisfactory position.

He determined, however, to extract a promise from her before giving in.

"I will consent, Nellie, on the condition that you stop seeing this fellow Fairfax and riding around in his big green car. I won't stand for that."

Nellie smiled, more to herself than to him. She had Fairfax in the meshes. He was safe. The man was madly in love with her. The instant she was freed from Harvey he stood ready to become her husband—Fairfax, with all his money and all his power.

And that is precisely what she was aiming at. She could afford to smile, but somehow she was coming to feel that this little man who was now her husband had it in him, after all, to put up a fierce and desperate fight for his own. If he were pushed to the wall he would fight back like a wildcat, and well she knew that there would be disagreeable features in the fray.

"If you are going to talk like that I'll never speak to you again," she said, banishing the smile. "Don't you trust me?"

"Sure," he said, and he meant it. "That's not the point."

"See here, Harve," she said, abruptly putting her hands on his shoulders and looking squarely into his eyes, "I want you to believe me when I say that I am a—a—well, a good woman."

"I believe it," he said, solemnly. Then, as an after-thought, "and I want to say the same thing for myself."

"I've never doubted you," said she, fervently. "Now, go home and let things stand as they are. Write to Mr. Davis to-night."

"I will. I say, won't you give me a kiss?"

59

She hesitated, still calculating.

"Yes, if you promise not to tell anybody," she said, with mock solemnity. As she expected, he took it seriously.

"Do you suppose I go 'round telling people I've kissed my wife?"

Then she gave him a peck on the cheek and let it go as a kiss.

"When will you be out to see us?"

"Soon, I hope," she said, quickly. "Now go, Harve, I'm going to lie down and rest. Kiss Phoebe for me."

He got to the door. She was fairly pushing him.

"I feel better," he said, taking a long breath.

"So do I," said she.

He paused for a moment to frown in some perplexity.

"Say, Nell, I left my cane in a street car coming down. Do you think it would be worth while to advertise for it?"

CHAPTER V

CHRISTMAS

The weeks went slowly by and Christmas came to the little house in Tarrytown. He had become resigned but not reconciled to Nellie's continued and rather persistent absence, regarding it as the sinister proclamation of her intention to carry out the plan for separation in spite of all that he could do to avert the catastrophe. His devotion to Phoebe was more intense than ever; it had reached the stage of being pathetic.

True to his word, he wrote to Mr. Davis, who in time responded, saying that he could give him a place at the soda fountain in May, but that the wages would of necessity be quite small, owing to the fact that the Greeks had invaded Blakeville with the corner fruit stands and soft-drink fountains. He could promise him eight dollars a week, or ten dollars if he would undertake to come to the store at six A.M. and sweep up, a task now performed by the proprietor himself, who found himself approaching an age and a state of health that craved a feast of luxury and ease hitherto untasted.

Harvey was in considerable doubt as to his ability to live on ten dollars a week and support Phoebe, as well as to begin the task of reimbursing Nellie for her years of sacrifice. Still, it was better than nothing at all, so he accepted Mr. Davis' ten-dollar-a-week offer and sat back to wait for the coming of the first of May.

In the meantime he would give Nellie some return for her money by doing the work now performed by Annie—or, more advisedly speaking, a portion of it. He would conduct Phoebe to the kindergarten and call for her at the close of sessions, besides dressing her in the morning, sewing on buttons for her, undressing her at night, and all such jobs as that, with the result that Annie came down a dollar a week in her wages and took an extra afternoon out. In this way he figured he could save Nellie at least thirty dollars. He also did the janitor's work about the place and looked after the furnace, creating a salvage of three dollars and a half a month. Moreover, instead of buying a new winter suit and replacing his shabby ulster with one more comely and presentable, he decided to wear his fall suit until January and then change off to his old blue serge spring suit, which still seemed far from shiny, so far as he could see.

And so it was that Nellie's monthly check for $150 did very nicely.

Any morning at half-past eight, except Sunday, you could have seen him going down the street with Phoebe at his side, her hand in his, bound for the kindergarten. He carried her little lunch basket and whistled merrily when not engaged in telling her about Santa Claus. She startled him one day by asking:

"Are you going to be Santy this year, daddy, or is mamma?"

He looked down at the rich little fur coat and muff Nellie had outfitted her with, at the expensive hat and the silk muffler, and sighed.

"If you ask questions, Santy won't come at all," he said, darkly. "He's a mighty cranky old chap, Santy is."

He did not take up physical culture with Professor Flaherty, partly on account of the expense, partly because he found that belabouring cannel coal and shaking down the furnace was more developing than he had expected. Raking the autumn leaves out of the front yard also was harder than he had any idea it would be. He was rather glad it was not the season for the lawn mower.

Down in his heart he hoped that Nellie would come out for Christmas, but he knew there was no chance of it. She would have two performances on that day. He refrained from telling Phoebe until the very last minute that her mother would not be out for the holiday. He hadn't the heart to do it.

He broke the news then by telling the child that her mother was snowbound and couldn't get there. An opportune fall of snow the day before Christmas gave him the inspiration.

He set up the little Christmas tree in the back parlour, assisted by Bridget and Annie, after Phoebe had gone to bed on Christmas Eve. She had urged him to read to her about Tiny Tim, but he put her off with the announcement that Santa was likely to be around early on account of the fine sleighing, and if he saw that she wasn't asleep in bed he might skip the house entirely.

The expressman, in delivering several boxes from town that afternoon, had said to his helper:—

"That little fellow that came to the door was Nellie Duluth's husband, Mr.— Mr.—Say, look on the last page there and see what his name is. He's a cheap skate. A dime! Wot do you think of that?" He held up the dime Harvey had given him and squinted at it as if it were almost too small to be seen with the naked eye.

Nellie sent "loads" of presents to Phoebe—toys, books, candies, fruits, pretty dresses, a velvet coat, a tiny pair of opera glasses, strings of beads, bracelets, rings—dozens of things calculated to set a child mad with delight. There were pocketbooks, handkerchiefs, squirrel stoles and muffs for each of the servants, a box of cigars for the postman, another for the milkman, and a five-dollar bill for the janitor.

There was nothing for Harvey.

He looked for a long time at the envelope containing the five-dollar bill, an odd little smile creeping into his eyes. He was the janitor, he remembered. After a moment of indecision he slipped the bill into another envelope, which he marked "Charity" and laid aside until morning brought the mendicant who, with bare fingers and frosted lips, always came to play his mournful clarionet in front of the house.

Surreptitiously he searched the two big boxes carefully, inwardly hoping that she had not forgotten—nay, ignored—him. But there was nothing there, not even a Christmas card! It was the first Christmas she had....

The postman brought a small box addressed to Phoebe. The handwriting was strange, but he thought nothing of it. He thought it was nice of Butler to remember his little one and lamented the fact that he had not bought something for the little Butlers, of whom there were seven. He tied a red ribbon around the sealed package and hung it on the tree.

After it was all over he went upstairs and tried to read "Dombey & Son." But a mist came over his blue eyes and his vision carried him far beyond the printed page. He was not thinking of Nellie, but of his old mother, who had never forgotten to send him a Christmas present. Ah, if she were alive he would not be wondering to-night why Santa Claus had passed him by.

He rubbed his eyes with his knuckles, closed "Dombey & Son" for the night, and went to bed, turning his thoughts to the row of tiny stockings that hung from the mantelpiece downstairs—for Phoebe had put to use all that she could find—and then let them drift on through space to an apartment near Central Park, where Kris Kringle had delivered during the day a little packet containing the brooch he had purchased for his wife out of the money he had preserved from the sale of his watch some weeks before.

He was glad he had sent Nellie a present.

Bright and early the next morning he was up to have a final look at the tree before Phoebe came down. A blizzard was blowing furiously; the windows were frosted; the house was cheerless. He built the fires in the grates and sat about with his shoulders hunched up till the merry crackle of the coals put warmth into his veins. The furnace! He thought of it in time, and hurried to the basement to replenish the fires. They were out. He had forgotten them the night before. Bridget found him there later on, trying to start the kindling in the two furnaces.

"I clean forgot 'em last night," he said, sheepishly.

"I don't wonder, sor," said Bridget, quite genially for a cold morning. "Do you be after going upstairs this minute, sor. I'll have them roaring in two shakes av a lamb's tail. Mebby there's good news for yez up there. Annie's at the front door this minute, taking a telegram from the messenger bye, sor. Merry Christmas to ye, sor."

"Merry Christmas, Bridget!" cried he, gaily. His heart had leaped at the news she brought. A telegram from Nellie! Hurrah! He rushed upstairs without brushing the coal dust from his hands.

The boy was waiting for his tip. Harvey gave him a quarter and wished him a merry Christmas.

"A miserable day to be out," said he, undecided whether to ask the half-frozen lad to stay and have a bite of breakfast or to let him go out into the weather.

"It's nothin' when you gets used to it," said the blue-capped philosopher, and took his departure.

"But it's the getting used to it," said Harvey to Annie as she handed him the message. He tore open the envelope. She saw the light die out of his eyes.

The message was from Ripton, the manager, and read:—

"Please send Phoebe in with the nurse to see the matinée to-day."

The invitation was explicit enough. He was not wanted.

If he had a secret inclination to ignore the command altogether, it was frustrated by his own short-sightedness. He gulped, and then read the despatch aloud for the benefit of the maid. When it was too late he wished he had not done so.

Annie beamed. "Oh, sir, I've always wanted to see Miss Duluth act. I will take good care of Phoebe."

He considered it beneath his dignity to invite her into a conspiracy against the child, so he gloomily announced that he would go in with them on the one-o'clock train and stay to bring them out.

The Christmas tree was a great success. Phoebe was in raptures. He quite forgot his own disappointment in watching her joyous antics. As the distributor of the presents that hung on the gaily trimmed and dazzling cedar, he came at last to the little package from Butler. It contained a beautiful gold chain, at the end of which hung suspended a small diamond-studded slipper— blue enamel, fairly covered with rose diamonds.

Phoebe screamed with delight. Her father's face was a study.

"Why, they are diamonds!" he murmured. "Surely Butler wouldn't be giving presents like this." A card fluttered to the floor. He picked it up and read:—"A slipper for my little Cinderella. Keep it and it will bring good luck."

There was no name, but he knew who had sent it. With a cry of rage he snatched the dainty trinket from her hand and threw it on the floor, raising his foot to stamp it out of shape with his heel. His first vicious attempt missed the slipper altogether, and before he could repeat it the child was on the floor clutching it in her fingers, whimpering strangely. The servants looked on in astonishment.

He drew back, mumbling something under his breath. In a moment he regained control of himself.

"It—it isn't meant for you, darling," he said, hoarsely. "Santy left it here by mistake. We will send it back to him. It belongs to some other poor little girl."

"But I am Cinderella!" she cried. "Mr. Fairy-fax said so. He told Santy to bring it to me. Please, daddy—please!"

He removed it gently from her fingers and dropped it into his pocket. His face was very white.

"Santy isn't that kind of a man," he said, without rhyme or reason. "Now, don't cry, dearie. Here's another present from mamma. See!"

Later in the morning, after she had quite forgotten the slipper, he put it back in the box, wrapped it carefully, and addressed the package to L. Z. Fairfax, in New York City, without explanation or comment.

Phoebe

Before the morning was half over he was playing with Phoebe and her toys quite as childishly and gleefully as she, his heart in the fun she was having, his mind almost wholly cleared of the bitterness and rancour that so recently had filled it to overflowing.

The three of them floundered through the snowdrifts to the station, laughing and shouting with a merriment that proved infectious. The long-obscured sun came out and caught the disease, for he smiled broadly, and the wind gave over snarling and smirked with an amiability that must have surprised the shivering horses standing desolate in front of certain places wherein their owners partook of Christmas cheer that was warm.

Harvey took Phoebe and the nurse to the theatre in a cab. He went up to the box-office window and asked for the two tickets. The seller was most agreeable. He handed out the little envelope with the words:—

"A packed house to-day, Mr.—Mr.—er—ah, and—sold out for to-night. Here you are, with Miss Duluth's compliments—the best seats in the house. And here is a note for—er—yes, for the nurse."

Annie read the note. It was from Nellie, instructing her to bring Phoebe to her dressing-room after the performance, where they would have supper later on.

Harvey saw them pass in to the warm theatre and then slowly wandered out to the bleak, wind-swept street. There was nothing for him to do; nowhere that he could go to seek cheerful companions. For an hour or more he wandered up and down Broadway, his shoulders hunched up, his mittened hands to his ears, water running from his nose and eyes, his face the colour of the setting sun. Half-frozen, he at last ventured into a certain café, a place where he had lunched no fewer than half-a-dozen times, and where he thought his identity might have remained with the clerk at the cigar stand.

There were men at the tables, smoking and chatting hilariously. At one of them sat three men, two of whom were actors he had met. Summoning his courage, he approached them with a well-assumed air of nonchalance.

"Merry Christmas," was his greeting. The trio looked at him with no sign of recognition. "How are you. Mr. Brackley? How are you, Joe?"

The two actors shook hands with him without much enthusiasm, certainly without interest.

Light dawned on one of them. "Oh," said he, cheerlessly, "how are you? I couldn't place you at first." He did not offer to introduce him to the stranger, but proceeded to enlighten the other players. "It's—oh, you know—Nellie Duluth's husband."

The other fellow nodded and resumed his conversation with the third man. At the same time the speaker leaned forward to devote his attention to the tale in hand, utterly ignoring the little man, who stood with his hand on the back of the vacant chair.

Harvey waited for a few moments. "What will you have to drink?" he asked, shyly dropping into the chair. They stared at him and shook their heads.

"That seat's engaged," said the one called "Joe," gruffly.

Harvey got up instantly. "Oh," he said, in a hesitating manner. They went on with their conversation as if he were not there. After a moment he moved away, his ears burning, his soul filled with mortification and shame. In a sort of daze he approached the cigar stand and asked for a box of cigarettes.

"What kind?" demanded the clerk, laying down his newspaper.

Harvey smiled engagingly. "Oh, the kind I usually get!" he said, feeling sure that the fellow remembered him and the quality he smoked.

"What's that?" snapped the clerk, scowling.

The purchaser hastily mentioned a certain kind of cigarette, paid for it after the box had been tossed at him, and walked away. Fixed in his determination to stay in the place until he was well thawed out, he took a seat at a little table near the stairway and ordered a hot lemonade.

He was conscious of a certain amount of attention from the tables adjacent to the trio he had accosted. Several loud guffaws came to his ears as he sipped the boiling drink. Taking an unusually copious swallow, he coughed and spluttered as the liquid scalded his tongue and palate. The tears rushed to his eyes. From past experience he knew that his tongue would be sore for at least a week. He had such a tender tongue, Nellie said.

For half an hour he sat there dreaming and brooding. It was much better than tramping the streets. A clock on the opposite wall pointed to four o'clock. The matinée would be over at a quarter to five. Presently he looked again. It was five minutes past four. Really it wasn't so bad waiting after all; not half so bad as he had thought it would be.

Some one tapped him on the shoulder. He looked up with a start. The manager of the place stood at his elbow.

"This isn't a railway station, young feller," he said, harshly. "You'll have to move on. These tables are for customers."

"But I've bought—"

"Now, don't argue about it. You heard what I said. Move along."

The man's tone was peremptory. Poor Harvey looked around as if in search of a single benevolent face, and then, without a word of protest, arose and moved quickly toward the door. His eyes were fixed in a glassy stare on the dancing, elusive doorway. He wondered if he could reach it before he sank through the floor. Somehow he had the horrible feeling that just as he opened it to go out some one would kick him from behind. He could almost feel the impact of the boot and involuntarily accelerated his speed as he opened the door to pass into the biting air of the now darkening street.

"I hate this damned town," said he to himself over and over again as he flung himself against the gale that almost blew him off his feet. When he stopped to take his bearings, he was far above Longacre Square and still going in the wrong direction. He was befuddled. A policeman told him in hoarse, muffled tones to go back ten blocks or so if he wanted to find the theatre where Nellie Duluth was playing.

A clock in an apothecary's shop urged him to hurry. When he came to the theatre, the newsboys were waiting for the audience to appear. He was surrounded by a mob of boys and men shouting the extras.

"Is the show out?" he asked one of them.

"No, sir!" shouted the boy, eagerly. "Shall I call up your automobile, mister!"

"No, thank you," said Harvey through his chattering teeth. For a moment he felt distinctly proud and important. So shrewd a judge of humanity as a New York "newsy" had taken him to be a man of parts. For awhile he had been distressed by the fear, almost the conviction, that he was regarded by all New York as a "jay."

Belying his suddenly acquired air of importance, he hunched himself up against the side of the building, partly sheltered from the wind, and waited for the crowd to pour forth. With the appearance of the first of those home-goers he would repair to the stage door, and, once behind the scenes, was quite certain that he would receive an invitation from Nellie to join the gay little family supper party in her dressing-room.

When the time came, however, he approached the doorman with considerable trepidation. He had a presentiment that there would be "no admittance." Sure enough, the grizzled doorman, poking his head out, gruffly informed him that no one was allowed "back" without an order from the manager. Harvey explained who he was, taking it for granted that the man did not know him with his coat-collar turned up.

"I know you, all right," said the man, not unkindly. "I'd like to let you in, but —you see—" He coughed and looked about rather helplessly, avoiding the pleading look in the visitor's eyes.

"It's all right," Nellie's husband assured him, but an arm barred the way.

"I've got strict orders not to admit you," blurted out the doorman, hating himself.

"Not to admit me!" said Harvey, slowly.

"I'm sorry, sir. Orders is orders."

"But my little girl is there."

"Yes, sir, I understand. The orders are for you, sir, not for the kid." Struck by the look in the little man's eyes he hastened to say, "Maybe if you saw Mr. Ripton out front and sent a note in to Miss Duluth, she'd change her mind and—"

"Good Lord!" fell from Harvey's lips as he abruptly turned away to look for a spot where he could hide himself from every one.

Two hours later, from his position at the mouth of the alley, he saw a man come out of the stage door and blow a whistle thrice. He was almost perishing with cold; he was sure that his ears were frozen. A sharp snap at the top of each of them and a subsequent warmth urged him to press quantities of snow against them, obeying the old rule that like cures like. From the kitchens of a big restaurant came the odours of cooking foodstuffs. He was hungry on this Merry Christmas night, but he would not leave his post. He had promised to wait for Phoebe and take her out home with him in the train.

With the three blasts of the whistle he stirred his numb feet and edged nearer to the stage door. A big limousine came rumbling up the alley from behind, almost running him down. The fur-coated chauffeur called him unspeakable names as he passed him with the emergency brakes released.

Before he could reach the entrance, the door flew open and a small figure in fur coat and a well known white hat was bundled into the machine by a burly stage hand. A moment later Annie clambered in, the door was slammed and the machine started ahead.

He shouted as he ran, but his cry was not heard. As the car careened down the narrow lane, throwing snow in all directions, he dropped into a dejected, beaten walk. Slowly he made his way in the trail of the big car—it was too dark for him to detect the colour, but he felt it was green—and came at last to the mouth of the alley, desolate, bewildered, hurt beyond all understanding.

For an instant he steadied himself against the icy wall of a building, trying to make up his mind what to do next. Suddenly it occurred to him that if he ran hard and fast he could catch the train—the seven-thirty—and secure a bit of triumph in spite of circumstances.

He went racing up the street toward Sixth Avenue, dodging head-lowered pedestrians with the skill of an Indian, and managed to reach Forty-second Street without mishap or delay. Above the library he was stopped by a policeman, into whose arms he went full tilt, almost bowling him over. The impact dazed him. He saw many stars on the officer's breast. As he looked they dwindled into one bright and shining planet and a savage voice was bellowing:—

"Hold still or I'll bat you over the head!"

"I'm—I'm trying to make the seven-thirty," he panted, wincing under the grip on his arm.

"We'll see about that," growled the policeman.

"For Heaven's sake, Mr. Policeman, I haven't done anything. Honest, I'm in a hurry. My little girl's on that train. We live in Tarrytown. She'll cry her eyes out if I—"

"What was you running for?"

"For it," said Harvey, at the end of a deep breath.

"It's only seven-five now," said the officer, suspiciously.

"Well, it's the seven-ten I want, then," said Harvey, hastily.

"I guess I'll hold you here and see if anybody comes chasin' up after you. Not a word, now. Close your trap."

As no one came up to accuse the prisoner of murder, theft, or intoxication, the intelligent policeman released him at the expiration of fifteen minutes. A crowd had collected despite the cold. Harvey was always to remember that crowd of curious people; he never ceased wondering where they came from and why they were content to stand there shivering in the zero weather when there were stoves and steam radiators everywhere to be found. To add to his humiliation at least a dozen men and boys, not satisfied with the free show as far as it had gone, pursued him to the very gates in the concourse.

"Darned loafers!" said Harvey, hotly, but under his breath, as he showed his ticket and his teeth at the same time. Then he rushed for the last coach and swung on as it moved out.

Now, if I were inclined to be facetious or untruthful I might easily add to his troubles by saying that he got the wrong train, or something of the sort, but it is not my purpose to be harder on him than I have to be.

It was the right train, and, better still, Annie and Phoebe were in the very last seat of the very last coach. With a vast sigh he dropped into a vacant seat ahead of them and began fanning himself with his hat, to the utter amazement of onlookers, who had been disturbed by his turbulent entrance.

The newspaper Annie was reading fell from her hands.

"My goodness, sir! Where did you come from?" she managed to inquire.

"I've been—dining—at—Sherry's," he wheezed. "Annie, will you look and see if my ears are frozen?"

"They are, sir. Good gracious!"

He realised that he had been indiscreet.

"I—I sat in a draught," he hastened to explain. "Did you have a nice time, Phoebe?"

The child was sleepy. "No," she said, almost sullenly. His heart gave a bound. "Mamma wouldn't let me eat anything. She said I'd get fat."

"You had quite enough to eat, Phoebe," said Annie.

"I didn't," said Phoebe.

"Never mind," said her father, "I'll take you to Sherry's some day."

"When, daddy?" she cried, wide awake at once. "I like to go to places with you."

He faltered. "Some day after mamma has gone off on the road. We'll be terribly gay, while she's away, see if we ain't."

Annie picked up the paper and handed it to him.

"Miss Duluth ain't going on the road, sir," she said. "It's in the paper."

He read the amazing news. Annie, suddenly voluble, gave it to him by word of mouth while he read. It was all there, she said, to prove what she was telling him. "Just as if I couldn't read!" said Harvey, as he began the article all over again after perusing the first few lines in a perfectly blank state of mind.

"Yes, sir, the doctor says she can't stand it on the road. She's got nervous prosperity and she's got to have a long rest. That Miss Brown is going to take her place in the play after this week and Miss Duluth is going away out West to live for awhile to get strong again. She—What is the name of the town, Phoebe?"

"Reno," said Phoebe, promptly.

"But the name of the town isn't in the paper, sir," Annie informed him. "It's a place where people with complications go to get rid of them, Miss Nellie says. The show won't be any good without her, sir. I wouldn't give two cents to see it."

He sagged down in the seat, a cold perspiration starting out all over his body.

"When does she go—out there!" he asked, as in a dream.

"First of next week. She goes to Chicago with the company and then right on out to—to—er—to—"

"Reno," said he, lifelessly.

"Yes, sir."

He did not know how long afterward it was that he heard Phoebe saying to him, her tired voice barely audible above the clacking of the wheels:—

"I want a drink of water, daddy."

His voice seemed to come back to him from some far-away place. He blinked his eyes several times and said, very wanly:—

"You mustn't drink water, dearie. It will make you fat."

CHAPTER VI

THE REVOLVER

He waited until the middle of the week for some sign from her; none coming, he decided to go once more to her apartment before it was too late. The many letters he wrote to her during the first days after learning of her change of plans were never sent. He destroyed them. A sense of shame, a certain element of pride, held them back. Still, he argued with no little degree of justice, there were many things to be decided before she took the long journey —and the short step she was so plainly contemplating.

It was no more than right that he should make one last and determined effort to save her from the fate she was so blindly courting. It was due her. She was his wife. He had promised to cherish and protect her. If she would not listen to the appeal, at least he would have done his bounden duty.

There was an ever present, ugly fear, too, that she meant, by some hook or crook, to rob him of Phoebe.

"And she's as much mine as hers," he declared to himself a thousand times or more.

Behind everything, yet in plain view, lay his own estimate of himself—the naked truth—he was "no good!" He had come to the point of believing it of himself. He was not a success; he was quite the other thing. But, granting that, he was young and entitled to another chance. He could work into a partnership with Mr. Davis if given the time.

Letting the midweek matinée slip by, he made the plunge on a Thursday. She was to leave New York on Sunday morning; that much he knew from the daily newspapers, which teemed with Nellie's breakdown and its lamentable consequences. It would be at least a year, the papers said, before she could resume her career on the stage. He searched the columns daily for his own name, always expecting to see himself in type little less conspicuous than that accorded to her, and stigmatised as a brute, an inebriate, a loafer. It was all the same to him—brute, soak, or loafer. But even under these extraordinary conditions he was as completely blanketed by obscurity as if he never had been in existence.

Sometimes he wondered whether she could get a divorce without according him a name. He had read of fellow creatures meeting death "at the hand of a person (or of persons) unknown." Could a divorce complaint be worded in such non-committal terms? Then there was that time-honoured shroud of private identity, the multitudinous John Doe. Could she have the heart to bring proceedings against him as John Doe? He wondered.

If he were to shoot himself, so that she might have her freedom without going to all the trouble of a divorce or the annoyance of a term of residence in Reno, would she put his name on a tombstone? He wondered.

A strange, a most unusual thing happened to him just before he left the house to go to the depot. He was never quite able to account for the impulse which sent him upstairs rather obliquely to search through a trunk for a revolver, purchased a couple of years before, following the report that housebreakers were abroad in Tarrytown, and which he had promptly locked away in his trunk for fear that Phoebe might get hold of it.

He rummaged about in the trunk, finally unearthing the weapon. He slipped it into his overcoat pocket with a furtive glance over his shoulder. He chuckled as he went down the stairs. It was a funny thing for him to do, locking the revolver in the trunk that way. What burglar so obliging as to tarry while he went through all the preliminaries incident to destruction under the circumstances? Yes, it was stupid of him.

He did not consider the prospect of being arrested for carrying concealed weapons until he was halfway to the city, and then he broke into a mild perspiration. From that moment he eyed every man with suspicion. He had heard of "plain clothes men." They were the very worst kind. "They take you unawares so," said he to himself, with which he moved closer to the wall of the car, the more effectually to conceal the weapon. It wouldn't do to be caught going about with a revolver in one's pocket. That would be the very worst thing that could happen. It would mean "the Island" or some other such place, for he could not have paid a fine.

It occurred to him, therefore, that it would be wiser to get down at One Hundred and Tenth street and walk over to Nellie's. The policemen were not so thick nor so bothersome up there, he figured, and it was a rather expensive article he was carrying; one never got them back from the police, even if the fine were paid.

Footsore, weary, and chilled to the bone, he at length came to the apartment building wherein dwelt Nellie Duluth. In these last few weeks he had developed a habit of thinking of her as Nellie Duluth, a person quite separate and detached from himself. He had come to regard himself as so far removed from Nellie Duluth that it was quite impossible for him to think of her as Mrs. —Mrs.—he had to rack his brain for the name, the connection was so remote.

He had walked miles—many devious and lengthening miles—before finally coming to the end of his journey. Once he came near asking a policeman to direct him to Eighty-ninth Street, but the sudden recollection of the thing he carried stopped him in time. That and the discovery of a sign on a post which frostily informed him that he was then in the very street he sought.

It should go without the saying that he hesitated a long time before entering the building. Perhaps it would be better after all to write to her. Somewhat sensibly he argued that a letter would reach her, while it was more than likely he would fall short of a similar achievement. She couldn't deny Uncle Sam, but she could slam the door in her husband's face. Yes, he concluded, a letter was the thing. Having come to this half-hearted decision, he proceeded to argue himself out of it. Suppose that she received the letter, did it follow that she would reply to it? He might enclose a stamp and all that sort of thing, but he knew Nellie; she wouldn't answer a letter—at least, not that kind of letter. She would laugh at it, and perhaps show it to her friends, who also would be vastly amused. He remembered some of them as he saw them in the café that day; they were given to uproarious laughter. No, he concluded, a letter was not the thing. He must see her. He must have it out with her, face to face.

So he went up in the elevator to the eleventh floor, which was the top one, got out and walked down to the sixth, where she lived. Her name was on the door plate. He read it three or four times before resolutely pressing the electric button. Then he looked over his shoulder quickly, impelled by the queer feeling that some one was behind him, towering like a dark, threatening shadow. A rough hand seemed ready to close upon his shoulder to drag him back and down. But no one was there. He was alone in the little hall. And yet something was there. He could feel it, though he could not see it; something sinister that caused him to shiver. His tense fingers relaxed their grip on the revolver. Strangely the vague thing that disturbed him departed in a flash and he felt himself alone once more. It was very odd, thought he.

Rachel came to the door. She started back in surprise, aye, alarm, when she saw the little man in the big ulster. A look of consternation sprang into her black eyes.

He opened his lips to put the natural question, but paused with the words unuttered. The sound of voices in revelry came to his ears from the interior of the apartment, remote but very insistent. Men's voices and women's voices raised in merriment. His gaze swept the exposed portion of the hall. Packing boxes stood against the wall, piled high. The odour of camphor came out and smote his sense of smell.

Rachel was speaking. Her voice was peculiarly hushed and the words came quickly, jerkily from her lips.

"Miss Duluth is engaged, sir. I'm sorry she will not be able to see you."

He stared uncertainly at her and beyond her.

"So she's packing her things," he murmured, more to himself than to the servant. Rachel was silent. He saw the door closing in his face. A curious sense of power, of authority, came over him. "Hold on," he said sharply, putting his foot against the door. "You go and tell her I want to see her. It's important—very important!"

"She has given orders, sir, not to let you—"

"Well, I'm giving a few orders myself, and I won't stand for any back talk, do you hear? Who is the master of this place, tell me that?" He thumped his breast with his knuckles. "Step lively, now. Tell her I'm here."

He pushed his way past her and walked into what he called the "parlour," but what was to Nellie the "living-room." Here he found numerous boxes, crates, and parcels, all prepared for shipment or storage. Quite coolly he examined the tag on a large crate. The word "Reno" smote him. As he cringed he smiled a sickly smile without being conscious of the act. "Wait a minute," he called to Rachel, who was edging in an affrighted manner toward the lower end of the hall and the dining-room. "What is she doing?"

Rachel's face brightened. He was going to be amenable to reason.

"It's a farewell luncheon, sir. She simply can't be disturbed. I'll tell her you were here."

"You don't need to tell her anything," said he, briskly. The sight of those crates and boxes had made another man of him. "I'll announce myself. She won't—"

"You'd better not!" cried Rachel, distractedly. "There are some men here. They will throw you out of the apartment. They're big enough, Mr.—Mr.—"

He grinned. His fingers took a new grip on the revolver.

"Napoleon wasn't as big as I am," he said, much to Rachel's distress. It sounded very mad to her. "Size isn't everything."

"For Heaven's sake, sir, please don't—"

"They seem to be having a gay old time," said he, as a particularly wild burst of laughter came from the dining-room. He hesitated. "Who is out there?"

Rachel was cunning. "I don't know the names, sir. They're—they're strangers to me."

At that instant the voice of Fairfax came to his ears, loudly proclaiming a health to the invalid who was going to Reno. Harvey stood there in the hall, listening to the toast. He heard it to the end, and the applause that followed. If he were to accept the diagnosis of the speaker, Nellie was repairing to Reno to be cured of an affliction that had its inception seven years before, a common malady, but not fatal if taken in time. The germ, or, more properly speaking, the parasite, unlike most bacteria, possessed but two legs, and so on and so forth.

The laughter was just dying away when Harvey—who recognised himself as the pestiferous germ alluded to—strode into the room, followed by the white-faced Rachel.

"Who was it, Rachel?" called out Nellie, from behind the enormous centrepiece of roses which obstructed her view of the unwelcome visitor.

The little man in the ulster piped up, shrilly:—

"She don't know my name, but I guess you do, if you'll think real hard."

There were ten at the table, flushed with wine and the exertion of hilarity. Twenty eyes were focussed on the queer, insignificant little man in the doorway. If they had not been capable of focussing them on anything a moment before, they acquired the power to do so now.

Nellie, staring blankly, arose. She wet her lips twice before speaking.

"Who let you in here?" she cried, shrilly.

One of the men pushed back his chair and came to his feet a bit unsteadily.

"What the deuce is it, Nellie?" he hiccoughed.

Nellie had her wits about her. She was very pale, but she was calm. Instinctively she felt that trouble—even tragedy—was confronting her; the thing she had feared all along without admitting it even to herself.

"Sit down, Dick," she commanded. "Don't get excited, any of you. It's all right. My husband, that's all."

The man at her right was Fairfax. He was gaping at Harvey with horror in his face. He, too, had been expecting something like this. Involuntarily he shifted his body so that the woman on the other side, a huge creature, was partially between him and the little man in the door.

"Get him out of here!" he exclaimed. "He's just damned fool enough to do something desperate if we—"

"You shut up!" barked Harvey, in a sudden access of fury. "Not a word out of you, you big bully."

"Get him out!" gasped Fairfax, holding his arm over his face. "What did I tell you? He's crazy! Grab him, Smith! Hurry up!"

"Grab him yourself!" retorted Smith, in some haste. "He's not gunning for me."

What there was to be afraid of in the appearance of the little ulstered man who stood there with his hands in his pockets I cannot for the life of me tell, but there was no doubt as to the consternation he produced in the midst of this erstwhile jovial crowd. An abrupt demand of courtesy urged him to raise his hand to doff his hat in the presence of ladies. Twenty terrified eyes watched the movement as if ten lives hung on the result thereof. Half of the guests were standing, the other half too petrified to move. A husband is a thing to strike terror to the heart, believe me, no matter how trivial he may be, especially an unexpected husband.

"Go away, Harvey!" cried Nellie, placing Fairfax between herself and the intruder.

"Don't do that!" growled the big man, sharply. "Do you suppose I want him shooting holes through me in order to get at you?"

"Is he going to shoot?" wailed one of the women, dropping the wineglass she had been holding poised near her lips all this time. The tinkle of broken glass and the douche of champagne passed unnoticed. "For God's sake, let me get out of here!"

"Keep your seats, ladies and gents," said Harvey, hastily, beginning to show signs of confusion. "I just dropped in to see Nellie for a few minutes. Don't let me disturb you. She can step into the parlour, I guess. They'll excuse you, Nellie."

"I'll do nothing of the sort," snapped Nellie, noting the change in him. "Go away or I'll have a policeman called."

He grinned. "Well, if you do, he'll catch me with the goods," he said, mysteriously.

"The goods?" repeated Nellie.

"Do you want to see it?" he asked, fixing her with his eyes. As he started to withdraw his hand from his overcoat pocket, a general cry of alarm went up and there was a sudden shifting of positions.

"Don't do that!" roared two or three of the men in a breath.

"Keep that thing in your pocket!" commanded Fairfax, huskily, without removing his gaze from the arm that controlled the hidden hand.

Harvey gloated. He waved the hand that held his hat. "Don't be alarmed, ladies," he said. "You are quite safe. I can hit a silver dollar at twenty paces, so there's no chance of anything going wild."

"For God's sake!" gasped Fairfax. Suddenly he disappeared beneath the edge of the table. His knees struck the floor with a resounding thump.

"Get away from me!" shrieked the corpulent lady, kicking at him as she fled the danger spot.

Harvey stooped and peered under the table at his enemy, a broad grin on his face. Fairfax took it for a grin of malevolence.

"Peek-a-boo!" called Harvey.

"Don't shoot! For the love of Heaven, don't shoot!" yelled Fairfax. Then to the men who were edging away in quest of safety behind the sideboard, china closet, and serving table:—"Why don't you grab him, you idiots?"

Harvey suddenly realised the danger of his position. He straightened up and jerked the revolver from his pocket, brandishing it in full view of them all.

"Keep back!" he shouted—a most unnecessary command.

Those who could not crowd behind the sideboard made a rush for the butler's pantry. Feminine shrieks and masculine howls filled the air. Chairs were overturned in the wild rush for safety. No less than three well-dressed women were crawling on their hands and knees toward the only means of exit from the room.

"Telephone for the police!" yelled Fairfax, backing away on all-fours, suggesting a crawfish.

"Stay where you are!" cried Harvey, now thoroughly alarmed by the turn of affairs.

They stopped as if petrified. The three men who were wedged in the pantry door gave over struggling for the right of precedence and turned to face the peril.

Once more he brandished the weapon, and once more there were shrieks and groans, this time in a higher key.

Nellie alone stood her ground. She was desperate. Death was staring her in the face, and she was staring back as if fascinated.

"Harvey! Harvey!" she cried, through bloodless lips. "Don't do it! Think of Phoebe! Think of your child!"

Rachel was stealing down the hall. The little Napoleon suddenly realised her purpose and thwarted it.

"Come back here!" he shouted. The trembling maid could not obey for a very excellent reason. She dropped to the floor as if shot, and, failing in the effort to crawl under a low hall-seat, remained there, prostrate and motionless.

He then addressed himself to Nellie, first cocking the pistol in a most cold-blooded manner. Paying no heed to the commands and exhortations of the men, or the whines of the women, he announced:—

"That's just what I've come here to ask you to do, Nellie; think of Phoebe. Will you promise me to—"

"I'll promise nothing!" cried Nellie, exasperated. She was beginning to feel ridiculous, which was much worse than feeling terrified. "You can't bluff me, Harvey, not for a minute."

"I'm not trying to bluff you," he protested. "I'm simply asking you to think. You can think, can't you? If you can't think here with all this noise going on, come into the parlour. We can talk it all over quietly and—why, great Scott, I don't want to kill anybody!" Noting an abrupt change in the attitude of the men, who found some encouragement in his manner, he added hastily, "Unless I have to, of course. Here, you! Don't get up!" The command was addressed to Fairfax. "I'd kind of like to take a shot at you, just for fun."

"Harvey," said his wife, quite calmly, "if you don't put that thing in your pocket and go away I will have you locked up as sure as I'm standing here."

"I ask you once more to come into the parlour and talk it over with me," said he, wavering.

"And I refuse," she cried, furiously.

"Go and have it out with him, Nellie," groaned Fairfax, lifting his head above the edge of the table, only to lower it instantly as Harvey's hand wabbled unsteadily in a sort of attempt to draw a bead on him.

"Well, why don't you shoot?" demanded Nellie, curtly.

"No! No!" roared Fairfax.

"No! No!" shrieked the women.

"For two cents I would," stammered Harvey, quite carried away by the renewed turmoil.

"You would do anything for two cents," said Nellie, sarcastically.

"I'd shoot myself for two cents," he wailed, dismally. "I'm no use, anyway. I'd be better off dead."

"For God's sake let him do it, Nellie," hissed Fairfax. "That's the thing; the very thing."

Poor Harvey suddenly came to a full realisation of the position he was in. He had not counted on all this. Now he was in for it, and there was no way out of it. A vast sense of shame and humiliation mastered him. Everything before him turned gray and bleak, and then a hideous red.

He had not meant to do a single thing he had already done. Events had shaped themselves for him. He was surprised, dumfounded, overwhelmed. The only thought that now ran through his addled brain was that he simply had to do something. He couldn't stand there forever, like a fool, waving a pistol. In a minute or two they would all be laughing at him. It was ghastly. The wave of self-pity, of self-commiseration submerged him completely. Why, oh why, had he got himself into this dreadful pickle? He had merely come to talk it over with Nellie, that and nothing more. And now, see what he was in for!

"By jingo," he gasped, in the depth of despair, "I'll do it! I'll make you sorry, Nellie; you'll be sorry when you see me lying here all shot to pieces. I've been a good husband to you. I don't deserve to die like this, but—" His watery blue eyes took in the horrified expressions on the faces of his hearers. An innate sense of delicacy arose within him. "I'll do it in the hall."

"Be careful of the rug," cried Nellie, gayly, not for an instant believing that he would carry out the threat.

"Shall I do it here?" he asked, feebly.

"No!" shrieked the women, putting their fingers in their ears.

"By all means!" cried Fairfax, with a loud laugh of positive relief.

To his own as well as to their amazement, Harvey turned the muzzle of the pistol toward his face. It wabbled aimlessly. Even at such short range he had the feeling that he would miss altogether and looked over his shoulder to see if there was a picture or anything else on the wall that might be damaged by the stray bullet. Then he inserted the muzzle in his mouth.

Stupefaction held his audience. Not a hand was lifted, not a breath was drawn. For half a second his finger clung to the trigger without pressing it. Then he lowered the weapon.

"I guess I better go out in the hall, where the elevator is," he said. "Don't follow me. Stay where you are. You needn't worry."

"I'll bet you ten dollars you don't do it," said Fairfax, loudly, as he came to his feet.

"I don't want your dirty money, blast you," exclaimed Harvey, without thinking. "Good-by, Nellie. Be good to Phoebe. Tell 'em out in Blakeville that I—oh, tell 'em anything you like. I don't give a rap!"

He turned and went shambling down the hall, his back very stiff, his ears very red.

It was necessary to step over Rachel's prostrate form. He got one foot across, when she, crazed with fear, emitted a piercing shriek and arose so abruptly that he was caught unawares. What with the start the shriek gave him and the uprising of a supposedly inanimate mass, his personal equilibrium was put to the severest test. Indeed, he quite lost it, going first into the air with all the sprawl of a bronco buster, and then landing solidly on his left ear where there wasn't a shred of rug to ease the impact. In a twinkling, however, he was on his feet, apologising to Rachel. But she was crawling away as fast as her hands and knees would carry her. From the dining-room came violent shouts, the hated word "police" dominating the clamour.

He slid through the door and closed it after him. A moment later he was plunging down the steps, disdaining the elevator, which, however fast it may have been, could not have been swift enough for him in his present mood. The police! They would be clanging up to the building in a jiffy, and then what? To the station house!

Half-way down he paused to reflect. Voices above came howling down the shaft, urging the elevator man to stop him, to hold him, to do all manner of things to him. He felt himself trapped.

So he sat down on an upper step, leaned back against the marble wall, closed his eyes tightly, and jammed the muzzle of the revolver against the pit of his stomach.

"I hate to do it," he groaned, and then pulled the trigger.

The hammer fell with a sharp click. He opened his eyes. If it didn't hurt any more than that he could do it with them open. Why not? In a frenzy to have it over with he pulled again and was gratified to find that the second bullet was not a whit more painful than the first. Then he thought of the ugly spectacle he would present if he confined the mutilation to the abdominal region. People would shudder and say, "how horrible he looks!" So he considerately aimed the third one at his right eye.

Even as he pulled the trigger, and the hammer fell with the usual click, his vision centred on the black little hole in the end of the barrel. Breathlessly he waited for the bullet to emerge. Then, all of a sudden, he recalled that there had been no explosion. The fact had escaped him during the throes of a far from disagreeable death. He put his hand to his stomach. In a dumb sort of wonder he first examined his fingers, and, finding no gore, proceeded to a rather careful inspection of the weapon.

Then he leaned back and dizzily tried to remember when he had taken the cartridges out of the thing.

"Thank the Lord," he said, quite devoutly. "I thought I was a goner, sure. Now, when did I take 'em out?"

The elevator shot past him, going upward. He paid no attention to it.

It all came back to him in a flash. He remembered that he had never loaded it at all. A loaded pistol is a very dangerous thing to have about the house. The little box of cartridges that came with the weapon was safely locked away at the bottom of the trunk, wrapped in a thick suit of underwear for protection against concussion.

Even as he congratulated himself on his remarkable foresight the elevator, filled with excited men, rushed past him on the way down. He heard them saying that a dangerous lunatic was at large and that he ought to be—But he couldn't hear the rest of it, the car being so far below him.

"By jingo!" he exclaimed, leaping to his feet in consternation. "They'll get me now. What a blamed fool I was!"

Scared out of his wits, he dashed up the steps, three at a jump, and, before he knew it, ran plump into the midst of the women who were huddled at Nellie's landing, waiting for the shots and the death yells from below. They scattered like sheep, too frightened to scream, and he plunged through the open door into the apartment.

"Where are you, Nellie?" he bawled. "Hide me! Don't let 'em get me. Nellie! Oh, Nellie!"

The shout would have raised the dead. Nellie was at the telephone. She dropped the receiver and came toward him.

"Aren't you ashamed of yourself!" she squealed, clutching his arm. "What an awful spectacle you've made of yourself—and me! You blithering little idiot. I—"

"Where can I hide?" he whispered, hopping up and down in his eagerness. "Hurry up! Under a bed or—anywhere. Good gracious, Nellie, they'll get me sure!"

She slammed the door.

"I ought to let them take you and lock you up," she said, facing him. The abject terror in his eyes went straight to her heart. "Oh, you poor thing!" she cried, in swift compassion. "You—you wouldn't hurt a fly. You couldn't. Come along! Quick! I'll do this much for you, just this once. Never again! You can get down the back steps into the alley if you hurry. Then beat it for home. And never let me see your face again."

Three minutes later he was scuttling down the alley as fast as his eager legs could carry him.

Nellie was holding the front door against the thunderous assault of a half dozen men, giving him time to escape. All the while she was thinking of the depositions she could take from the witnesses to his deliberate attempt to kill her. He had made it very easy for her.

CHAPTER VII

THE LAWYER

He was dismally confident that he would be arrested and thrown into jail on Friday. It was always an unlucky day for him. The fact that Nellie had aided and abetted in his undignified flight down the slippery back steps did not in the least minimise the peril that still hung like a cloud over his wretched head. Of course, he understood: she was sorry for him. It was the impulse of the moment. When she had had time to think it all over and to listen to the advice of Fairfax and the others, she would certainly swear out a warrant.

As a measure of precaution he had slyly tossed the revolver from a car window somewhere north of Spuyten Duyvil, and, later on at home, stealthily disposed of the box of cartridges.

All evening long he sat huddled up by the fireplace, listening with all ears for the ominous sound of constabulary thumpings at the front door. The fierce wind shrieked around the corners of the house, rattling the shutters and banging the kitchen gate, but he heard nothing, for his own heart made such a din in response to the successive bursts of noise that all else seemed still by comparison.

His efforts to amuse the perplexed Phoebe were pitiful. The child took him to task for countless lapses of memory in his recital of oft-told and familiar fairy tales.

But no one came that night. And Friday, too, dragged itself out of existence without a sign from Nellie or the dreaded officers of the law. You may be sure he did not poke his nose outside the door all that day. Somehow he was beginning to relish the thought that she would be gone on Sunday, gone forever, perhaps. He loved her, of course, but distance at this particular time was not likely to affect the enchantment. In fact, he was quite sure he would worship her a great deal more comfortably if she were beyond the border of the State.

The thought of punishment quite overshadowed a previous dread as to how he was going to provide for Phoebe and himself up to the time of assuming the job in Davis' drug store. He had long since come to the conclusion that if Nellie persisted in carrying out her plan to divorce him he could not conscientiously accept help from her, nor could he expect to retain custody of the child unless by his own efforts he made suitable provision for her. His one great hope in the face of this particular difficulty had rested on the outcome of the visit to her apartment, the miserable result of which we know. Not only had he upset all of his fondest calculations, but he had heaped unthinkable ruin in the place he had set aside for them.

There was nothing consoling in the situation, no matter how he looked at it. More than once he regretted the emptiness of that confounded cylinder. If there had been a single bullet in the thing his troubles would now be over. Pleasing retrospect! But not for all the money in the world would he again subject himself to a similar risk.

It made him shudder to even think of it. It was hard enough for him to realise that he had had the monumental courage to try it on that never to be forgotten occasion. As a matter of fact, he was rather proud of it, which wouldn't have been at all possible if he had succeeded in the cowardly attempt.

Suppose, thought he with a qualm—suppose there had been a bullet! It was now Saturday. His funeral would be held on Saturday. By Saturday night he would be in a grave—a lonesome, desolate grave. Nellie would have seen to that, so that she could get away on Sunday. Ugh! It was most unpleasant!

The day advanced. His spirits were rising. If nothing happened between then and midnight he was reasonably secure from arrest.

But in the middle of the day the blow fell. Not the expected blow, but one that stunned him and left him more miserable than anything else in the world could have done.

There came a polite knock at the door. Annie admitted a pleasant-faced, rather ceremonious young man, who said he had business of the utmost importance to transact with Mr.—Mr.—He glanced at a paper which he drew from his pocket, and supplying the name asked if the gentleman was in.

Harvey was tiptoeing toward the dining-room, with Phoebe at his heels, when the stranger entered the library.

"Pardon me," called the young man, with what seemed to Harvey unnecessary haste and emphasis. "Just a moment, please!"

Harvey stopped, chilled to the marrow.

"It was all a joke," he said, quickly. "Just a little joke of mine. Ha! Ha!" It was a sepulchral laugh.

"I am John Buckley, from the offices of Barnes & Canby, representing Miss Duluth, your wife, I believe? It isn't a pleasant duty I have to perform Mr.—Mr—er—but, of course, you understand we are acting in the interests of our client and if we can get together on this—"

"Can't you come some other day?" stammered Harvey, holding Phoebe's hand very tightly in his. "I'm—I'm not well to-day. We—we are waiting now for the health officer to—to see whether it's smallpox or just a rash of—"

The pleasant young gentleman laughed.

"All the more necessary why we should settle the question at once. If it is smallpox the child would be quarantined with you—that would be unfortunate. You don't appear to have a rash, however."

"It hasn't got up to my face yet," explained Harvey, feebly. "You ought to see my body. It's—"

"I've had it," announced the young man, glibly; "so I'm immune." He winked.

"What do you want?" demanded Harvey, bracing himself for the worst. "Out with it. Let's see your star."

"Oh, I'm not a cop. I'm a lawyer."

The other swallowed noisily.

"A lawyer?"

"We represent Miss Duluth. I'll get down to tacks right away, if you'll permit me to sit down." He took a chair.

"Tacks?" queried Harvey, a retrospective grin appearing on his lips. "Gee! I wish I'd thought to put a couple—But, excuse me, I can't talk without my lawyer being present."

The visitor stared. "You—do you mean to say you have retained counsel?"

"The best in New York," lied Harvey.

Buckley gave a sigh of relief. He knew a lie when he heard one.

"I'd suggest that you send the little girl out of the room. We can talk better if we are alone."

After Phoebe's reluctant departure, the visitor bluntly asked Harvey which he preferred, State's prison or an amicable adjustment without dishonour.

"Neither," said Harvey, moistening his lips.

Thereupon Mr. Buckley calmly announced that his client, Miss Duluth, was willing to forego the pleasure of putting him behind the bars on condition that he surrendered at once the person of their child—their joint child, he put it, so that Harvey might not be unnecessarily confused—to be reared, educated, and sustained by her, without let or hindrance, from that time forward, so on and so forth; a bewildering rigmarole that meant nothing to the stupefied father, who only knew that they wanted to take his child away from him.

"Moreover," said Mr. Buckley, "our client has succeeded in cancelling the lease on this cottage and has authorised the owner to take possession on the first of the month—next Wednesday, that is. Monday morning, bright and early, the packers and movers will be here to take all of her effects away. Tuesday night, we hope, the house will be quite empty and ready to be boarded up. Of course, Mr.—Mr.—er—, you will see to it that whatever trifling effects you may have about the place are removed by that time. After that, naturally, little Miss Phoebe will be homeless unless provision is made for her by—er—by the court. We hope to convince you that it will be better for her if the question is not referred to a court of justice. Your own good sense will point the alternative. Do I make myself quite clear to you?"

"No," said Harvey, helplessly.

"Well, I'll be a little more explicit," said the lawyer, grimly. "A warrant will be issued for your arrest before two o'clock to-day if you do not grasp my meaning before that hour. It is twelve-ten now. Do you think you can catch the idea in an hour and fifty minutes?"

Harvey was thoughtful. "What is the smallest sentence they can give me if I —if I stand trial?"

"That depends," said Mr. Buckley, slightly taken aback, but without submitting an explanation. "You don't want to bring disgrace on the child by being branded as a jailbird, do you?"

"Nellie won't have the heart to put me in jail," groaned the unhappy little man. "She—she just can't do it. She knows I'd die for her. She—"

"But she isn't the State of New York," explained her counsel, briskly. "The State hasn't anything in the shape of a heart. Now, I'm here to settle the matter without a contest, if that's possible. If you want to fight, all right. You know just what you'll get. Besides, isn't it perfectly clear to you that Miss Duluth doesn't want to put you in jail? That's her idea, pure and simple. I don't mind confessing that our firm insisted for a long time on giving you up to the authorities, but she wouldn't have it that way. She wants her little girl, that's all. Isn't that perfectly fair?"

"She's—she's going to give up the house?" murmured Harvey, passing his hand over his eyes.

"Certainly."

"It's a mighty inconvenient time for us to—to look for another place—"

"That's just what I've been saying to you," urged Buckley. "The Weather

Bureau says we'll have zero weather for a month or two. I shudder to think of that poor child out in—"

"Oh, Lord!" came almost in a wail from the lips of Phoebe's father. He covered his face with his hands. Mr. Buckley, unseen, smiled triumphantly.

At four o'clock Phoebe, with all her childish penates, was driven to the station by Mr. Buckley, who, it would appear, had come prepared for the emergency. Before leaving he gave the two servants a month's wages and a two weeks' notice dating from the 18th of December and left with Harvey sufficient money to pay up all the outstanding bills of the last month—with a little left over.

We draw a curtain on the parting that took place in the little library just before the cab drove away.

Phoebe was going to Reno.

Long, long after the departure her father lifted his half-closed blue eyes from the coals in the grate and discovered that the room was ice-cold.

He understood the habits of astute theatrical managers so well by this time that he did not have to be told that the company would journey to Chicago by one of the slow trains. The comfort and convenience of the player is seldom considered by the manager, who, as a rule, when there is time to spare, transports his production by the least expensive way. Harvey knew that Nellie and the "Up in the Air" company would pass through Tarrytown on the pokiest day train leaving New York over the Central. There was, of course, the possibility that the affluent Nellie might take the eighteen-hour train, but it was somewhat remote.

Sunday morning found him at the Tarrytown station, awaiting the arrival or the passing of the train bearing the loved ones who were casting him off. He was there early, bundled in his ulster, an old Blakeville cap pulled down over his ears, a limp cigarette between his lips. A few of the station employés knew him and passed the time of day.

"Going in rather early, ain't you, Mr.—Mr.—" remarked the station master, clapping his hands to generate warmth.

"No," said Harvey, leaving the inquirer in the dark as to whether he referred to a condition or a purpose.

A couple of hours and a dozen trains went by. Harvey, having exhausted his supply of cigarettes, effected the loan of one from the ticket agent.

"Waiting for some one, sir?" asked that worthy. "Or are you just down to see the cars go by?"

"What time does the Chicago train go through?" asked Harvey.

"Any particular one?"

"No; I'm not particular."

"There's one at eleven-forty."

"I'm much obliged."

He was panic-stricken when the train at last appeared and gave unmistakable signs of stopping at Tarrytown. Moved by an inexplicable impulse, he darted behind a pile of trunks. His dearest hope had been that Phoebe might be on the lookout for him as the cars whizzed through, and that she would waft a final kiss to him. But it was going to stop! He hadn't counted on that. It was most embarrassing.

From his hiding place he watched the long line of sleepers roll by, slower and slower, until with a wheeze they came to a full stop. His eager eyes took in every window that passed. There was no sign of Phoebe. Somewhat emboldened, he ventured forth from shelter and strolled along the platform for a more deliberate scrutiny of the windows.

The feeling of disappointment was intense. He had never known loneliness so great as this which came to him now. The droop to his shoulders became a little more pronounced as he turned dejectedly to re-enter the waiting-room. The train began to move out as he neared the corner of the building. The last coach crept by. He watched it dully.

A shrill cry caught his ear. His eyes, suddenly alert, focussed themselves on the observation platform of the private car as it picked up speed and began the diminishing process. Braced against the garish brass bars that enclosed the little platform was Phoebe, in her white fur coat and hood, her mittened fingers clutching the rail, above which her rosy face appeared as the result of eager tiptoeing. The excellent Rachel stood behind the child, cold and unsmiling.

"Hello, daddy!" screamed Phoebe, managing to toss him a kiss, just as he had hoped and expected.

The response cracked in his throat. It was a miserable croak that he sent back, but he blew her a dozen kisses.

"Good-bye, daddy!" came the shrill adieu, barely audible above the clatter of the receding train.

He stood quite still until the last coach vanished up the track. The tears on his cheeks were frozen.

Some one was speaking to him.

"Ain't you going West with 'em, Mr.—, Mr.—?" queried the baggage master.

Harvey gazed at him dumbly for a moment or two. Then he lifted his chin.

"I—I've got to wait over a few days to see to the packing and storing of my household effects," he said, briskly. Then he trudged up the hill.

Sure enough, the packers appeared "bright and early" Monday morning, just as Buckley had said they would. By nine o'clock the house was upside down and by noon it was full of excelsior, tar paper, and crating materials. The rasp of the saw and the bang of the hammer resounded throughout the little cottage. Burly men dragged helpless and unresisting articles of furniture about as if they had a personal grudge against each separate piece, and pounded them, and drove nails into them, and mutilated them, and scratched them, and splintered them, and after they were completely conquered marked their pine board coffins with the name "Nellie Duluth," after which they were ready for the fireproof graveyard in Harlem.

Dazed and unsteady, Harvey watched the proceedings with the air of one who superintends. He gave a few instructions, offered one or two suggestions— principally as to the state of the weather—and was on the jump all day long to keep out of the way of the energetic workmen. He had seen Marceline at the Hippodrome on one memorable occasion. Somehow he reminded himself of the futile but nimble clown, who was always in the way and whose good intentions invariably were attended by disaster.

The foreman of the gang, doubtless with a shrewd purpose in mind, opened half the windows in the house, thus forcing his men to work fast and furiously or freeze. Harvey almost perished in the icy draughts. He shut the front door fifty times or more, and was beginning to sniffle and sneeze when Bridget took pity on him and invited him into the kitchen. He hugged the cook stove for several hours, mutely watching the two servants through the open door of their joint bedroom off the kitchen while they stuffed their meagre belongings into a couple of trunks.

At last it occurred to him that it would be well to go upstairs and pack his own trunk before the workmen got to asking questions. He carried his set of Dickens upstairs, not without interrogation, and stored the volumes away at the bottom of his trunk. So few were his individual belongings that he was hard put to fill the trays compactly enough to prevent the shifting of the contents. When the job was done he locked the trunk, tied a rope around it and then sat down upon it to think. Had he left anything out? He remembered something. He untied the knots, unlocked the trunk, shifted half of the contents and put in his fishing tackle and an onyx clock Nellie had given him for Christmas two years before.

Later on he repeated the operation and made room for a hand saw, an auger, a plane, and a hatchet; also a smoking-jacket she had given him, and a lot of paper dolls Phoebe had left behind. (Late that night, after the lights were out, he remembered the framed motto, "God Bless Our Home," which his dear old mother had worked for him in yarns of variegated hues while they were honeymooning in Blakeville. The home was very cold and still, and the floor was strewn with nails, but he got out of bed and put the treasure in the top tray of the trunk.)

Along about four in the afternoon he experienced a sensation of uneasiness—even alarm. It began to look as if the workmen would have the entire job completed by nightfall. In considerable trepidation he accosted the foreman.

"If it's just the same to you I'd rather you wouldn't pack the beds until to-morrow—that is, of course, if you are coming back to-morrow."

"Maybe we'll get around to 'em and maybe we won't," said the foreman, carelessly. "We've got to pack the kitchen things to-morrow and the china."

"You see, it's this way," said Harvey. "I've got to sleep somewhere!"

"I see," said the foreman, and went on with his work, leaving Harvey in doubt.

"Have a cigar?" he asked, after a doleful pause. The man took it and looked at it keenly.

"I'll smoke it after a while," he said.

"Do the best you can about the bed in the back room upstairs," said Harvey, engagingly.

An express wagon came at five o'clock and removed the servants' trunks. A few minutes later the two domestics, be-hatted and cloaked, came up to say good-bye to him.

"You're not leaving to-day?" he cried, aghast.

"If it's just the same to you, sor," said Bridget. "We've both got places beginnin' to-morry."

"But who'll cook my—"

"Niver you worry about that, sor; I've left a dozen av eggs, some bacon, rolls, and—"

93

"All right. Good-bye," broke in the master, turning away.

"Good luck, sor," said Bridget, amiably. Then they went away.

His dismal reflections were broken by the foreman, who found him in the kitchen.

"We'll be back early in the morning and clean up everything. The van will be here at ten. Is everything here to go to the warehouse? I notice some things that look as though they might belong to you personally."

There were a few pieces of furniture and bric-à-brac that Harvey could claim as his own. He stared gloomily at the floor for a long time, thinking. Of what use were they to him now? And where was he to put them in case he claimed them?

"I guess you'd better store everything," he said, dejectedly. "They—they all go together."

"The—your trunk, sir; how about that?"

"If you think you've got room for it, I—"

"Sure we have."

"Take it, too. I'm going to pack what clothes I need in a suitcase. So much easier to carry than a trunk." He was unconsciously funny, and did not understand the well-meant guffaw of the foreman.

It was a dreary, desolate night that he spent in the topsy-turvy cottage. He was quite alone except for the queer shapes and shadows that haunted him. When he was downstairs he could hear strange whisperings above; when he was upstairs the mutterings were below. Things stirred and creaked that had never shown signs of animation before. The coals in the fireplace spat with a malignant fury, as if blown upon by evil spirits lurking in the chimney until he went to bed so that they might come forth to revel in the gloom. The howl of the wind had a different note, a wail that seemed to come from a child in pain; forbidding sounds came up from the empty cellar; always there was something that stood directly behind him, ready to lay on a ghostly hand. He crouched in the chair, feeling never so small, never so impotent as now. The chair was partially wrapped for crating. Every time he moved there was a crackle of paper that sounded like the rattle of thunder before the final ear-splitting crash. As still as a mouse he sat and listened for new sounds, more sinister than those that had gone before; and, like the mouse, he jumped with each recurring sound.

Towering crates seemed on the verge of toppling over upon him, boxes and barrels appeared to draw closer together to present a barrier against any means of escape; cords and ropes wriggled with life as he stared at them, serpentine things that kept on creeping toward him, never away.

Oh, for the sound of Phoebe's voice!

"Quoth the raven, nevermore!" That sombre sentence haunted him. He tried to close his ears against it, but to no purpose. It crept up from some inward lurking place in his being, crooning a hundred cadences in spite of all that he could do to change the order of his thoughts.

Far in the night he dashed fearfully up to his dismantled bedroom, a flickering candle in his hand. He had gone about the place to see that all of the doors and windows were fastened. Removing his shoes and his coat, he hurriedly crawled in between the blankets and blew out the light. Sleep would not come. He was sobbing. He got up twice and lighted the candle, once to put away the motto, again to take out of the trunk the cabinet size photograph of himself and Nellie and the baby, taken when the latter was three years old. Hugging this to his breast, he started back to bed.

A sudden thought staggered him. For a long time he stood in the middle of the room, shivering as he debated the great question this thought presented. At last, with a shudder, he urged his reluctant feet to carry him across the room to the single gas jet. Closing his eyes he turned on the gas full force and then leaped into the bed, holding the portrait to his heart. Then he waited for the end of everything.

When he opened his eyes broad daylight was streaming in upon him. Some one was pounding on the door downstairs. He leaped out of bed and began to pull on his shoes.

Suddenly it occurred to him that by all rights he should be lying there stiff and cold, suffocated by the escaping gas. He sniffed the air. There was no odour of gas. With a gasp of alarm he rushed over and turned off the stopcock, a cold perspiration coming out all over him.

"Gee, I hope I'm in time!" he groaned aloud. "I don't want to die. I—I—it's different in the daytime. The darkness did it. I hope I'm—" Then, considerably puzzled, he interrupted himself to turn the thing on again. He stood on his toes to smell the tip. "By jingo, I remember now, that fellow turned it off in the meter yesterday. Oh, Lord; what a close call I've had!"

He was so full of glee when he opened the door to admit the packers that they neglected, in their astonishment, to growl at him for keeping them standing in the cold for fifteen or twenty minutes.

"Thought maybe you'd gone and done it," said the foreman. "Took poison or turned on the gas, or something. You was mighty blue yesterday, Mr.—Mr.

Duluth."

With the arrival of the van he set off to pay the bills due the tradespeople in town, returning before noon with all the receipts, and something like $20 left over. The world did not look so dark and dreary to him now. In his mind's eye he saw himself rehabilitated in the sight of the scoffers, prospering ere long to such an extent that not only would he be able to reclaim Phoebe, but even Nellie might be persuaded to throw herself on his neck and beg for reinstatement in his good graces. With men like Harvey the ill wind never blows long or steadily; it blows the hardest under cover of night. The sunshine takes the keen, bitter edge off it, and it becomes a balmy zephyr.

Already he was planning the readjustment of his fortunes.

At length the van was loaded. His suitcase sat on the front porch, puny and pathetic. The owner of the house was there, superintending the boarding up of the windows and doors. Harvey stood in the middle of the walk, looking on with a strange yearning in his heart. All of his worldly possessions reposed in that humble bag, save the cotton umbrella that he carried in his hand. A cotton umbrella, with the mercury down to zero!

"Well, I'm sorry you're leaving," said the owner, pocketing the keys as he came up to the little man. "Can I give you a lift in my cutter down to the station?"

"If it isn't too much bother," said Harvey, blinking his eyes very rapidly.

"You're going to the city, I suppose."

"The city?"

"New York."

"Oh," said Harvey, wide-eyed and thoughtful, "I—I thought you meant Blakeville. I'm going out there for a visit with my Uncle Peter. He's the leading photographer in Blakeville. My mother's brother. No, I'm not going to New York. Not on your life!"

All the way to the station he was figuring on how far the twenty dollars would go toward paying his fare to Blakeville. How far could he ride on the cars, and how far would he have to walk? And what would his crabbed old uncle say to an extended visit in case he got to Blakeville without accident?

He bought some cigarettes at the newsstand and sat down to wait for the first train to turn up, westward bound.

CHAPTER VIII

BLAKEVILLE

If by any chance you should happen to stop off in the sleepy town of Blakeville, somewhere west of Chicago, you would be directed at once to the St. Nicholas Hotel, not only the leading hostelry of the city, but—to quote the advertisement in the local newspaper—the principal hotel in that Congressional district. After you had been conducted to the room with a bath —for I am sure you would insist on having it if it were not already occupied, which wouldn't be likely—you would cross over to the window and look out upon Main Street. Directly across the way you would observe a show window in which huge bottles filled with red, yellow, and blue fluids predominated. The sign above the door would tell you that it was a drug store, if you needed anything more illuminating than the three big bottles.

"Davis' drug store," you would say to your wife, if she happened to be with you, and if you have been at all interested in the history of Mr.—Mr.—Now, what is his name?—you would doubtless add, "It seems to me I have heard of the place before." And then you would stare hard to see if you could catch a glimpse of the soda-water dispenser, whose base of operations was just inside the door to the left, a marble structure that glistened with white and silver, and created within you at once a longing for sarsaparilla or vanilla and the delicious after effect of stinging gases coming up through the nostrils, not infrequently accompanied by tears of exquisite pain—a pungent pain, if you please.

At the rush periods of the day you could not possibly have seen him for the crowd of thirsty people who obstructed the view. Everybody in town flocked to Davis' for their chocolate sundaes and cherry phosphates. Was not Harvey behind the counter once more? With all the new-fangled concoctions from gay New York, besides a few novelties from Paris, and a wonderful assortment of what might well have been called prestidigitatorial achievements!

He had a new way of juggling an egg phosphate that was worth going miles to see, and as for the manner in which he sprinkled nutmeg over the surface— well! no Delsartian movement ever was so full of grace.

Yes, he was back at the old place in Davis'. For a year and a half he had been there. So prosperous was his first summer behind the "soda counter" that the owner of the place agreed with him that the fountain could be kept running all winter, producing hot chocolate, beef tea, and all that sort of thing. Just to keep the customers from getting out of the habit, argued Harvey in support of his plan—and his job.

You may be interested to learn how he came back to Blakeville. He was a fortnight getting there from Tarrytown. His railroad ticket carried him to Cleveland. From that city he walked to Chicago, his purpose being to save a few dollars so that he might ride into Blakeville. His feet were so sore and swollen when he finally hobbled into his Uncle Peter's art studio, on Main Street, that he couldn't get his shoes on for forty-eight hours after once taking them off. He confessed to a bit of high living in his time, lugubriously admitting to his uncle that he feared he had a touch of the gout. He was subject to it, confound it. Beastly thing, gout. But you can't live on lobster and terrapin and champagne without paying the price.

His uncle, a crusty and unimpressionable bachelor, was not long in getting the truth out of him. To Harvey's unbounded surprise the old photographer sympathised with him. Instead of kicking him out he took him to his bosom, so to speak, and commiserated with him.

"I feel just as sorry for a married man, Harvey," said he, "as I do for a half-starved dog. I'm always going out of my way to feed some of these cast-off dogs around town, so why shouldn't I do the same for a poor devil of a husband? I'll make you comfortable until you get into Davis', but don't you ever let on to these damned women that you're a failure, or that you're strapped, or that that measly little wife of yours gave you the sack. No, sir! Remember who you are. You are my nephew. I won't say as I'm proud of you, but, by thunder! I don't want anybody in Blakeville to know that I'm ashamed of you. If I feel that way about you, it's my own secret and it's nobody's business. So you just put on a bold front and nobody need know. You can be quite sure I won't tell on you, to have people saying that my poor dead sister's boy wasn't good enough for Ell Barkley or any other woman that ever lived.

"But it's a lesson to you. Don't—for God's sake, don't—ever let another one of 'em get her claws on you! Here's ten dollars. Go out and buy some ten-cent cigars at Rumley's, and smoke 'em where everybody can see you. Ten-centers, mind you; not two-fers, the kind I smoke. And get a new pair of shoes at Higgs'. And invite me to eat a—an expensive meal at the St. Nicholas. It can't cost more'n a dollar, no matter how much we order, but you can ask for lobster and terrapin, and raise thunder because they haven't got 'em, whatever they are. Then in a couple of days you can say you're going to help me out during the busy season, soliciting orders for crayon portraits. I'll board and lodge you here and give you four dollars a week to splurge on. The only thing I ask in return is that you'll tell people I'm a smart man for never having married. That's all!"

You may be quite sure that Harvey took to the place as a duck takes to water. Inside of a week after his arrival—or, properly speaking, his appearance in Blakeville, for you couldn't connect the two on account of the gout—he was the most talked-of, most envied man in the place. In the cigar stores, poolrooms, and at the St. Nicholas he was wont to regale masculine Blakeville with tales of high life in the Tenderloin that caused them to fairly shiver from attacks of the imagination, and subsequently to go home and tell their women folk what a gay Lothario he was, with the result that the interest in the erstwhile drug clerk spread to the other sex with such remarkable unanimity that no bit of gossip was complete without him. Every one affected his society, because every one wanted to hear what he had to say of the gay world on Manhattan Island; the life behind the scenes of the great theatres, the life in the million dollar cafés and hotels, the life in the homes of fashionable New Yorkers,—with whom he was on perfectly amiable terms,—the life in Wall Street. Some of them wanted to know all about Old Trinity, others were interested in the literary atmosphere of Gotham, while others preferred to hear about the fashions. But the great majority hungered for the details of convivial escapades—and he saw to it that they were amply satisfied. Especially were they interested in stories concerning the genus "broiler." Oh, he was really a devil of a fellow.

When the time came for him to begin his work as a solicitor for crayon portraits his reputation was such that not only was he able to gain admittance to every home visited, but he was allowed to remain and chat as long as he pleased, sometimes obtaining an order, but always being invited to call again after the lady of the house had had time to talk it over with her husband.

Sometimes he would lie awake in his bed trying in vain to remember the tales he had told and wondering if the people really believed him. Then he was prone to contrast his fiction with the truth as he knew it, and to blame himself for not having lived the brightly painted life when he had the opportunity. He almost wept when he thought of what he had missed. His imagination carried him so far that he cursed his mistaken rectitude and longed for one lone and indelible reminiscence which he could cherish as a real tribute to that beautiful thing called vice!

In answer to all questions he announced that poor Nellie had been advised to go West for her health. Of the real situation he said nothing.

No day passed that did not bring with it the longing for a letter from Nellie or a word from Phoebe. Down in his heart he was grieving. He wanted them, both of them. The hope that Nellie would appeal to him for forgiveness grew smaller as the days went by, and yet he did not let it die. His loyal imagination kept it alive, fed it with daily prayers and endless vistas of a reconstructed happiness for all of them.

Toward the end of his first summer at Davis' he was served with the notice that Nellie had instituted proceedings against him in Reno. It was in the days of Reno's early popularity as a rest cure for those suffering from marital maladies; impediments and complications were not so annoying as they appear to be in these latter times of ours. There was also a legal notice printed in the Blakeville *Patriot*.

The shock laid him up for a couple of days. If his uncle meant to encourage him by maintaining an almost incessant flow of invectives, he made a dismal failure of it. He couldn't convince the heartsick Harvey that Nellie was "bad rubbish" and that he was lucky to be rid of her. No amount of cajolery could make him believe that he was a good deal happier than he had ever been before in all his life; he wasn't happy and he couldn't be fooled into believing he was. He was miserable—desperately miserable. Looking back on his futile attempts to take his own life, he realised now that he had missed two golden chances to be supremely happy. How happy he could be if he were only dead! He was rather glad, of course, that he failed with the pistol, because it would have been such a gory way out of it, but it was very stupid of him not to have gone out pleasantly—even immaculately—by the other route.

But it was too late to think of doing it now. He was under contract with Mrs. Davis, Mr. Davis having passed on late in the spring, and he could not desert the widow in the midst of the busy season. His last commission as a crayon solicitor had come through Mrs. Davis, two months after the demise of Blakeville's leading apothecary. She ordered a life-size portrait of her husband, to be hung in the store, and they wept together over the prescription —that is to say, over the colour of the cravat and the shade of the sparse thatch that covered the head of the departed. Mrs. Davis never was to forget his sympathetic attitude. She never quite got over explaining the oversight that had deprived him of the distinction of being one of the pall-bearers, but she made up for it in a measure by insisting on opening the soda fountain at least a month earlier than was customary the next spring, and in other ways, as you will see later on.

Just as he was beginning to rise, phœnixlike, from the ashes of his despond, the *Patriot* reprinted the full details of Nellie's complaint as they appeared in a New York daily. For a brief spell he shrivelled up with shame and horror; he could not look any one in the face. Nellie's lawyers had made the astounding, outrageous charge of infidelity against him!

Infidelity!

He was stunned.

But just as he was on the point of resigning his position in the store, after six months of glorious triumph, the business began to pick up so tremendously that he wondered what had got into people.

His uncle chucked him in the ribs and called him a gay dog! Men came in and ordered sundaes who had never tasted one before, and they all looked at him in a strangely respectful way. Women smirked and giggled and called him a naughty fellow, and said they really ought not to let him wait on them.

All of a sudden it dawned on him that he was "somebody." He was a rake!

The New York paper devoted two full columns to his perfidious behaviour in the Tenderloin. For the first time in his life he stood in the limelight. Nellie charged him with other trifling things, such as failure to provide, desertion, cruelty; but none of these was sufficiently blighting to take the edge off the delicious clause which lifted him into the seventh heaven of a new found self-esteem! His first impulse had been to cry out against the diabolical falsehood, to deny the allegation, to fight the case to the bitter end. But on second thought he concluded to maintain a dignified silence, especially as he came to realise that he now possessed a definite entity not only in Blakeville, but in the world at large. He was a recognised human being! People who had never heard of him before were now saying, "What a jolly scamp he is! What a scalawag!" Oh, it was good to come into his own, even though he reached it by a crooked and heretofore undesirable thoroughfare. Path was not the word —it was a thoroughfare, lined by countless staring, admiring fellow creatures, all of whom pointed him out and called him by his own name.

Mothers cautioned their daughters, commanding them to have nothing to do with him, and then went with them to Davis' to see that the commands were obeyed. Fathers held him up to their sons as a dreadful warning, and then made it a point to drop in and tell him what they thought of him with a sly wink that pleased and never offended him.

He mildly protested against the sensational charge when questioned about it, saying that Nellie was mistaken, that her jealousy led her to believe a lot of things that were not true, and that he felt dreadfully cut up about the whole business, as it was likely to create a wrong impression in New York. Of course, he went on, no one in Blakeville believed the foolish thing! But in New York—well, they were likely to believe anything of a fellow there!

He moved in the very centre of a great white light. Reporters came in every day and asked him if there was anything new, hoping, of course, for fresh developments in the great divorce case. Lawyers dropped in to hint that they would like to take care of his interests. But there never was anything new, and his New York lawyers were perfectly capable of handling his affairs, particularly as he had decided to enter no general denial to the charges. He would let her get her divorce if she wanted it so badly as all that!

"I'd fight it," said the editor of the *Patriot*, counselling him one afternoon.

"You wouldn't if you had a child to consider," said Harvey, resignedly, quite overlooking the fact that there were nine growing children in the editor's household.

"She's too young to know anything about it," argued the other, earnestly.

Harvey shook his head. "You don't know what it is to be a father, Mr. Brinkley. It's a terrible responsibility."

Mr. Brinkley snorted. "I should say it is!"

"You'd think of your children if your wife sued you for divorce and charged you with—"

"I'd want my children to know I was innocent," broke in the editor, warmly.

"They wouldn't believe it if the lawyers got to cross-examining you," said Harvey, meaning well, but making a secret enemy of Mr. Brinkley, who thought he knew more of a regrettable visit to Chicago than he pretended.

Late in the fall several important epoch-making things happened to Harvey. Nellie was granted a divorce and the custody of the child. His uncle fell ill and died of pneumonia, and he found himself the sole heir to a thriving business and nearly three thousand dollars in bank. Mrs. Davis blandly proposed matrimony to him, now that he was free and she nearing the halfway stage of mourning.

He was somewhat dazed by these swift turns of the wheel of fate.

His first thought on coming into the fortune was of Phoebe, and the opportunities it laid open to him where she was concerned. His uncle had been dilatory in the matter of dying, but his nephew did not have it in his kindly heart to hold it up against the old gentleman. Still, if he had passed on a fortnight earlier, the decree might have been anticipated by a few days and Phoebe at least saved for him. Seeing that the poor old gentleman had to die anyway, it seemed rather inconsiderate of fate to put it off so long as it did. As it was, he would have to make the best of it and institute some sort of proceedings to get possession of the child for half of the year at the shortest.

He went so far as to slyly consult an impecunious lawyer about the matter, with the result that a long letter was sent to Nellie setting out the facts and proposing an amicable arrangement in lieu of more sinister proceedings. Harvey added a postscript to the lawyer's diplomatic rigmarole, conveying a plain hint to Nellie that, inasmuch as he was now quite well-to-do, she might fare worse than to come back to him and begin all over again.

The letter was hardly on its way to Reno, with instructions to forward, when he began to experience a deep and growing sense of shame; it was a pusillanimous trick he was playing on his poor old woman-hating uncle. Contemplating a resumption of the conjugal state almost before the old gentleman was cold in his grave! It was contemptible. In no little dread he wondered if his uncle would come back to haunt him. There was, at any rate, no getting away from the gruesome conviction, ludicrous as it may seem, that he would be responsible for the brisk turning over of Uncle Peter, if nothing more.

On top of this spell of uneasiness came the surprising proposition of Mrs. Davis. Between the suspense of not hearing from Nellie and the dread of offending the dead he was already in a sharp state of nerves. But when Mrs. Davis gently confided to him that she needed a live man to conduct her affairs without being actuated by a desire to earn a weekly salary he was completely stupefied.

"I'm afraid I don't understand, Mrs. Davis," he said, beginning to perspire very freely.

They were seated in the parlour of her house in Brown Street. She had sent for him.

"Of course, Harvey, it is most unseemly of me to suggest it at the present time, seeing as I have only been in mourning for three months, but I thought perhaps you'd feel more settled like if you knew just what to expect of me."

"Just what to expect?"

"Yes; so's you could rest easy in your mind. It would have to be quite a ways off yet, naturally, so's people wouldn't say mean things about us. They might, you know, considering the way you carried on with women in New York. Not for the world would I have 'em say or even think that anything had been going on between you and me prior to the time of Mr. Davis' death, but—but you know how people will talk if they get a chance. For that reason I think we'd better wait until the full period of mourning is over. That's only about a year longer, and it would stop—"

"Are—are you asking me to—to marry you, Mrs. Davis?" gasped Harvey, clutching the arms of the chair.

"Well, Harvey," said she, kindly, "I am making it easy for you to do it yourself."

"Holy—" began he, but strangled back the word "Mike," remembering that Mrs. Davis, a devout church member, abhorred anything that bordered on the profane.

"Holy what?" asked she, rather coyly for a lady who was not likely to see sixty again unless reincarnated.

"Matrimony," he completed, as if inspired.

"I know I am a few years older than you, Harvey, but you are so very much older than I in point of experience that I must seem a mere girl to you. We could—"

"Mrs. Davis, I—I can't do it," he blurted out, mopping his brow. "I suppose it means I'll lose my job in the store, but, honestly, I can't do it. I'm much obliged. It's awfully nice of you to—"

"Don't be too hasty," said she, composedly. "As I said in the beginning, I want some one to conduct the store in Mr. Davis' place. But I want that person to be part owner of it. No hired man, you understand? Now, how would a new sign over the door look, with your name right after Davis? Davis &—er—er—Oh, dear me!"

"I'll—I'll buy half of the store," floundered he. "I want to buy a half interest."

"I won't sell," said she, flatly. "I'm determined that the store shall never go out of the family while I am alive. There's only one way for you to get around that, and that's by becoming a part of the family."

"Why—why, Mrs. Davis, I'm only thirty years old. You surely don't mean to say you'd—you'd marry a kid like me? Let's see. My mother, if she was alive, wouldn't be as old as—"

"Never mind!" interrupted she, with considerable asperity. "We won't discuss your mother, if you please. Now, Harvey, don't be cruel. I am very fond of you. I will overlook all those scandalous things you did in New York. I can and will close my eyes to the wicked life you led there. I won't even ask their names—and that's more than most women would promise! I won't—"

"I can't do it," he repeated two or three times in rapid succession.

"Think it over, Harvey dear," said she, impressively.

"I'll buy a half interest if you'll let me, but I'll be doggoned if I'll marry a stepmother for Phoebe, not for the whole shebang!"

"Stepmother!" she repeated, shrilly. "I don't intend to be a stepmother!"

"Maybe I meant grandmother," he stammered in confusion. "I'm so rattled."

"Nellie has got Phoebe. She's not yours any longer. How can I be her stepmother? Answer that."

"You can't," said he, much too promptly.

"Well, promise me one thing, Harvey dear," she pleaded; "promise me you'll take a month or two to think it over. We couldn't be married for a year, in any event, so what's the sense of being in such a hurry to settle the matter definitely?"

Harvey reflected. He found himself in a very peculiar predicament. He had gone to her house with the avowed intention of offering her three thousand dollars and the studio in exchange for a half interest in the drug store. Now his long cherished dream seemed to be turning into a nightmare.

"I will think it over," he said, at last, in secret desperation. "But can't you give me a year's option?"

"On me?"

"On the store."

"Well, am I not the store?"

"No ma'am," said he, hastily. "I can't look at you in that light. I can't think of you as a drug store."

"I am sure I would make you a good and loving wife, Harvey. If Davis were alive he could tell you how devoted I was to him in all the—"

"But that's just the trouble, he isn't alive!" cried poor Harvey, at his wits' end. "Give me eight months."

"In the meantime you will up and marry some one else. Half the girls in town are crazy—no, I won't say that," she made haste to interrupt herself, suddenly realising the tactlessness of the remark. "Come up to dinner next Sunday and we will talk it over again. It is the best drug store in Blakeville, Harvey; remember that."

"I will remember it," he said, blankly, and took his departure.

As he passed Simpson's book store he dashed in and bought a New York dramatic paper. Hurriedly looking through the route list of companies, he found that the "Up in the Air" company was playing that week in Philadelphia. Without consulting his attorney he telegraphed to Nellie:—"Am in trouble. Uncle Peter is dead. Left me everything. Will you come back? Harvey."

The next day he had a wire from Nellie, charges collect:—"If he left you everything, why don't you pay for telegrams when you send them? Nellie."

He replied:—"I was not sure you were with the company, that's why. Shall I come to Philadelphia? Harvey."

Her answer:—"Not unless you are looking for more trouble. Nellie."

His next:—"There's a woman here who wants me to marry her. Won't you help me? Harvey."

Her last:—"There's a man here who is going to marry me. Why don't you marry her? Naughty! Naughty! Nellie."

He gave up in despair at this. On Sunday he allowed Mrs. Davis to bullyrag him into a tentative engagement. Then he began to droop. He had done a bit of investigating on his own account before going up to dine with her. She had been married to Davis forty-two years and then he died. If their only daughter had lived she would be forty-one years of age, and, if married, would doubtless be the mother of a daughter who might also in turn be the mother of a child. Figuring back, he made out that under these circumstances Mrs. Davis might very easily have been a great-grandmother. With this appalling thought in mind, he was quite firm in his determination to reject the old lady's proposal. Mrs. Davis taking Nellie's place! Pretty, gay, vivacious Nellie! It was too absurd for words.

But he went home an engaged man, just the same.

They were to be married in September of the following year, many months off.

That afternoon he saw a few gray hairs just above his ears and pulled them out. After that he looked for them every day. It was amazing how rapidly they increased despite his efforts to exterminate them. He began to grow careless in the matter of dress. His much talked of checked suits and lavender waistcoats took on spots and creases; his gaudy neckties became soiled and frayed; his fancy Newmarket overcoat, the like of which was only to be seen in Blakeville when some travelling theatrical troupe came to town, looked seedy, unbrushed, and sadly wrinkled. He forgot to shave for days at a time.

His only excuse to himself was, What's the use?

During the holidays, in the midst of a cheerful season of buying presents for Phoebe—and a bracelet for Nellie—he saw in the *Patriot*, under big headlines, the thing that served as the last straw for his already sagging back. The announcement was being made in all the metropolitan newspapers that "Nellie Duluth, the most popular and the most beautiful of all the comic opera stars," was to quit the stage forever on the first of the year to become the wife of "the great financier, L. Z. Fairfax, long a devoted admirer."

The happy couple were to spend the honeymoon on the groom's yacht, sailing in February for an extended cruise of the Mediterranean and other "sunny waters of the globe," primarily for pleasure but actually in the hope of restoring Miss Duluth to her normal state of health. A breakdown, brought on no doubt by the publicity attending her divorce a few months earlier, made it absolutely imperative, said the newspapers, for her to give up the arduous work of her chosen profession.

Harvey did not send the bracelet to her.

The long winter passed. Spring came and in its turn gave way to summer. September drew on apace. He went about with an ever increasing tendency to look at the wall calendar with a fixed stare when he should have been paying attention to the congratulations that came to him from the opposite side of the counter or showcase. His baby-blue eyes wore the mournful, distressed look of an offending dog; his once trim little moustache drooped over the corners of his mouth; his shoulders sagged and his feet shuffled as he walked.

"Harvey," said Mrs. Davis, not more than a fortnight before the wedding day, "You look terribly peaked. You must perk up for the wedding."

"I'm going into a decline," he said, affecting a slight cough.

"You are going to decline!" she shrilled, in her high, querulous voice.

"I said 'into,' Minerva," he explained, dully.

"I do believe I'm getting a bit deaf," she said, pronouncing it "deef."

"It will be mighty tough on you if I should suddenly go into quick consumption," said he, somewhat hopefully.

"You mustn't think of such a thing, dearie," she protested.

"No," said he, letting his shoulders sag again. "I suppose it's no use."

Just a week to the day before the 6th of September—the one numeral on the calendar he could see with his eyes closed—he shuffled over to the tailor's to try on the new Prince Albert coat and striped trousers that Mrs. Davis was giving him for a wedding present. He puffed weakly at the cigarette that hung from his lips and stared at the window without the slightest interest in what was going on outside.

A new train of thought was taking shape in his brain, as yet rather indefinite and undeveloped, but quite engaging as a matter for contemplation.

"Do you know how far it is to Reno?" he asked of the tailor, who paused in the process of ripping off the collar of the new coat.

"Couple of thousand miles, I guess. Why?"

"Oh, nothing," said Harvey, blinking his eyes curiously. "I just asked."

"You're not thinking of going out there, are you?"

"My health isn't what it ought to be," said Harvey, staring westward over the roof of the church down the street. "If I don't get better I may have to go West."

"Gee, is it as bad as all that?"

Harvey's lips parted to give utterance to a vigorous response, but he caught himself up in time.

"Maybe it won't amount to anything," he said, noncommittally. "I've got a little cough, that's all." He coughed obligingly, in the way of illustration.

"Don't wait too long," advised the kindly tailor. "If you get after it in time it can be checked, they say, although I don't believe it. In the family?"

"Not yet," said his customer, absently. "A week from to-day." A reflection which puzzled the tailor vastly.

Whatever may have been in Harvey's mind at the moment was swept away forever by the sudden appearance in the shop door of Bobby Nixon, the "boy" at Davis'.

"Say, Harvey," bawled the lad, "come on, quick! Mrs. Davis is over at the store and she's red-headed because you've been away for more'n an hour. She's got a telegram from some'eres and—"

"A telegram!" gasped Harvey, turning pale. "Who from?"

"How should I know?" shouted Bobby. "But she's got blood in her eye, you can bet on that."

Harvey did not wait for the tailor to strip the skeleton of the Prince Albert from his back, but dashed out of the shop in wild haste.

Mrs. Davis was behind the prescription counter. She had been weeping. At the sight of him she burst into fresh lamentations.

"Oh, Harvey, I've got terrible news for you—just terrible! But I won't put up with it! I won't have it! It's abominable! She ought to be tarred and feathered and—"

Harvey began to tremble.

"Somebody's doing it for a joke, Mrs. Davis," he gulped. "I swear to goodness I never had a thing to do with a woman in all my life. Nobody's got a claim on me, honest to—"

"What are you talking about, Harvey?" demanded Mrs. Davis, wide-eyed.

"What does it say?" cried he, pulling himself up with a jerk. "I'm innocent, whatever it is."

"It's from your wife," said Mrs. Davis, shaking the envelope in his face. "Read it! Read the awful thing!"

"From—from Nellie?" he gasped.

"Yes, Eller! Read it!"

"Hold it still! I can't read it if you jiggle it around—"

She held the envelope under his nose.

"Do you see who it's addressed to?" she grated out. "To me, as your wife. She thinks I'm already married to you. Read that name there, Harvey."

He read the name on the envelope in a sort of stupefaction. Then she whisked the message out and handed it to him, plumping herself down in a chair to fan herself vigorously while the prescription clerk hastened to renew his ministrations with the ammonia bottle, a task that had been set to him some time prior to the advent of Harvey.

Suddenly Harvey gave a squeal of joy and instituted a series of hops and bounds that threatened to create havoc in the narrow, bottle-encircled space behind the prescription wall. He danced up and down, waving the telegram on high, the tails of his half-finished wedding garment doing a mad obbligato to the tune of his nimble legs.

"Harvey!" shrieked Mrs. Davis, aghast.

"Yi-i-i!" rang out his ear-splitting yell. Pedestrians half a block away heard it and felt sorry for Mrs. Wiggs, the unhappy wife of the town sot, who, it went without saying, must be on another "toot."

"Harvey!" cried the poor lady once more.

"She's going to faint!" shouted the prescription clerk in consternation.

"Let her! Let her!" whooped Harvey. "It's all right, Joe! Let her faint if she wants to."

"I'm not going to faint!" exclaimed Mrs. Davis, struggling to her feet and pushing Joe away. "Keep quiet, Harvey! Do you want customers to think you're crazy? Give me that telegram. I'll attend to that. I'll answer it mighty quick, let me tell you. Give it to me."

Harvey sobered almost instantly. His jaw fell. The look in her face took all the joy out of his.

"Isn't—isn't it great, Minerva?" he murmured, as he allowed her to snatch the message from his unresisting fingers.

She glared at him. "Great? Why, you don't think for a moment that I'll have the brat in my house, do you? Great? I don't see what you can be thinking of, Harvey. You must be clean out of your head. I should say it ain't great. It's perfectly outrageous. Where's the telegraph office, Joe? I'll show the dreadful little wretch that she can't shunt her child off on me for support. Not much. Where is it, Joe? Didn't you hear what I asked?"

"Yes, ma'am," acknowledged Joe, blankly.

"You can't be mean enough—I should say you don't mean to tell her we won't take Phoebe?" gasped Harvey, blinking rapidly. "Surely you can't be so hard-hearted as all—"

"That will do, Harvey," said she, sternly. "Don't let me hear another word out of you. The idea! Just as soon as she thinks you're safely married to some one who can give that child a home she up and tries to get rid of her. The shameless thing! No, sir-ree! She can't shuffle her brat off on me. Not if I know what I'm—"

She fell back in alarm. The telegram fluttered to the floor. Harvey was standing in front of her, shaking his fist under her nose, his face contorted by a spasm of fury.

"Don't you call my little girl a brat," he sputtered. "And don't you dare to call my wife a shameless thing!"

"Your wife!" she gasped.

He waved his arms like a windmill.

"My widow, if you are going to be so darned particular about it," he shouted, inanely. "Don't you dare send a telegram saying Phoebe can't come and live with her father. I won't have it. She's coming just as fast as I can get her here. Hurray!"

Mrs. Davis lost all of her sternness. She dissolved into tears.

"Oh, Harvey dear, do you really and truly want that child back again?" she sniffled.

"Do I?" he barked. "My God, I should say I do! And say, I'd give my soul if I could get Nellie back, too. How do you like that?"

The poor woman was ready to fall on her knees to him.

"For Heaven's sake—for my sake—don't speak of such a thing. Don't try to get her back. Promise me! I'll let the child come, but—oh! don't take Nellie back. It would break my heart. I just couldn't have her around, not if I tried my—"

Harvey stared, open-mouthed. "I didn't mean that I'd like to have you take her back, Minerva. You haven't anything to do with it."

She stiffened. "Well, if I haven't, I'd like to know who has. It's my house, isn't it?"

"Don't make a scene, Minerva," he begged, suddenly aware of the presence of a curious crowd in the front part of the store. "Go home and I'll send the telegram. And say, if I were you, I'd go out the back way."

"And just to think, it's only a week till the wedding day," she choked out.

"We can put it off," he made haste to say.

"I know I shall positively hate that child," said she, overlooking his generous offer. "I will be a real stepmother to her, you mark my words. You can let her come if you want to, Harvey, but you mustn't expect me to treat her as anything but a—a—an orphan." She was a bit mixed in her nouns.

A brilliant idea struck him.

"You'd better be nice to her, Mrs. Davis, if you know what's good for you. Now, don't flare up! You mustn't forget you've broken the law by opening a telegram not intended for you."

"What?"

"It isn't addressed to you," he said, examining the envelope. "Your name is still Mrs. Davis, isn't it?"

"Of course it is."

"Well, then, what in thunder did you open a telegram addressed to my wife for? That's my wife's name, not yours."

"But," she began, vastly perplexed, "but it was meant for me."

"How do you know?" he demanded.

Her eyes bulged. "You—you don't mean that there is another one, Harvey?"

He winked with grave deliberateness. "That's for you to find out."

He darted through the back door into the alley, just as she collapsed in the prescriptionist's arms. In the telegraph office he read and re-read the message, his eyes aglow. It was from Nellie and came from New York, dated Friday, the first.

"Am sending Phoebe to Blakeville next Monday to make her home with you and Harvey. Letter to-day explains all. Have Harvey meet her in Chicago Tuesday, four P.M., Lake Shore."

He scratched his chin reflectively.

"I guess it don't call for an answer, after all," he said as much to himself as to the operator.

Nellie's letter came the next afternoon, addressed to Harvey. In a state of great excitement he broke the seal and read the poignant missive with eyes that were glazed with wonder and—something even more potent.

She began by saying that she supposed he was happily married, and wished him all the luck in the world. Then she came abruptly to the point, as she always did:—"I am in such poor health that the doctors say I shall have to go to Arizona at once. I am good for about six months longer at the outside, they say. Not half that long if I stay in this climate. Maybe I'll get well if I go out there. I'm not very keen about dying. I hate dead things; don't you? Now about Phoebe. She's been pining for you all these months. She doesn't like Mr. Fairfax, and he's not very strong for her. To be perfectly honest, he doesn't want her about. She's not his, and he hasn't much use for anything or anybody that doesn't belong to him. I've got so that I can't stand it, Harvey. The poor little kiddie is so miserably unhappy, and I'm not strong enough to get out and work for her as I used to. I would if I could. I think Fairfax is sick of the whole thing. He didn't count on me going under as I have. He hasn't been near me for a month, but he says it's because he hates the sight of Phoebe. I wonder. It wasn't that way a couple of years ago. But I'm different now. You wouldn't know me, I'm that thin and skinny. I hate the word, but that's what I am. The doctors have ordered me to a little place out in Arizona. I've got to do what they say, and what Fairfax says. It's the jumping-off place. So I'm leaving in a day or two with Rachel. My husband says he can't leave his business, but I'm not such a fool as he thinks. I won't say anything more about him, except that he hasn't the courage to watch me go down by inches.

"I can't leave Phoebe with him and I don't think it best to have her with me. She ought to be spared all that. She's so young, Harvey. She'd never forget. You love her, and she adores you. I'm giving her back to you. Don't—oh, please don't, ever let her leave Blakeville! I wish I had never left it, much as I hate it. I remember your new wife as being a kind, simple-hearted woman. She will be good to my little girl, I know, because she is yours as well. If I could get my health back, I'd work my heart out trying to support her, but it's out of the question. I have nothing to give her, Harvey, and I simply will not let Fairfax provide for her. Do you understand? Or are you as stupid and simple as you always were? And as tender-hearted?"

There was more, but Harvey's eyes were so full of tears he could not read.

He was waiting in the Lake Shore station when the train pulled in on Tuesday. His legs were trembling like two reeds in the wind and his teeth chattered with the chill of a great excitement. Out of the blur that obscured his vision bounded a small figure, almost toppling him over as it clutched his not too

113

stable legs and shrieked something that must have pleased him vastly, for he giggled and chortled like one gone daft with joy.

A soulless guard tapped him on the shoulder and gruffly ordered him to "get off to one side with the kid," he was blocking the exit—and flooding it, he added after a peep at Harvey's streaming eyes.

Rachel, tall and sardonic, stood patiently by until the little man recovered from his ecstasies.

"I thought you were staying with my—with Mrs. Fairfax," he said, gazing at her in amazement. He was holding Phoebe in his arms, and she was so heavy that his face was purple from the exertion.

"You'd better put her down," said Rachel, mildly. "She's not a baby any longer." With that she proceeded to pull the child's skirts down over the unnecessarily exposed pink legs. Harvey was not loath to set her down, a bit abruptly if the truth must be told. "Mrs. Fairfax is still in the drawing-room, sir. She doesn't want to get off until the crowd has moved out."

Harvey stared. "She's—on—the—train?"

"We change for the Santa Fe, which leaves this evening for the West. I'll go back to her now. The way is quite clear, I think. Good-bye, Phoebe. Be a good—"

He stopped, aghast, petrified

"I'm going with you!" cried Harvey, breathlessly. "Take me to the car."

Rachel hesitated. "You will be surprised, sir, when you see her. She's very frail, and—"

"Come on! Take me to my wife at once!"

"You forget, sir. She is not your wife any—"

"Oh, Lordy, Lordy!" fell dismally from his lips.

"And you have a new wife, I hear. So, if I were you, I'd avoid a scene if—"

But he was through the gate, dragging Phoebe after him. Rachel could not keep up with them. The eager little girl led him to the right car and he scurried up the steps, bursting into drawing-room B an instant later.

Nellie, wrapped in a thick garment, was lying back in the corner of the seat, her small, white face with its great dark eyes standing out with ghastly clearness against the collar of the ulster that almost enveloped her head.

He stopped, aghast, petrified.

"Oh, Nellie!" he wailed.

She betrayed no surprise. A wan smile transfigured her thin face. With an effort she extended a small gloved hand. He grasped it and found there was so little of it that it seemed lost in his palm. The sweat broke out on his forehead. He could not speak. This was Nellie!

Her voice was low and husky.

"Good-bye, Harvey. Be good to Phoebe, old fellow."

He choked up and could only nod his head.

"We can get out now, Mrs. Fairfax," said Rachel, appearing at the door. "Do you think you can walk, or shall I call for a—"

"Oh, I can walk," said Nellie, with a touch of her old raillery. "I'm not that far gone. Good-bye, Harvey. Didn't you hear me? Don't stand there watching me like that. It's bad enough without—"

He turned on Rachel furiously.

"Where is that damned Fairfax? Why isn't he here with her? The dog!"

"Hush, Harvey!"

"He's mean to mamma," broke in Phoebe, in her high treble. "I hate him. And so does mamma. Don't you, mamma?"

"Phoebe! Be quiet!"

"Where is he?" repeated Harvey, shaking his finger in Rachel's face.

"What are you blaming me for?" demanded the maid, indignantly. "Everybody blames me for everything. He's in New York, that's where he is. Now, you get out of here!"

She actually shoved him out into the aisle, where he stood trembling and uncertain, while she assisted her mistress to her feet and led her haltingly toward the exit.

Nellie looked back over her shoulder at him, quite coquettishly. She shook her head at him in mild derision.

"My, what a fire-eater my little Harvey has become," she said. He barely heard the words. "Your new wife must be scared half out of her wits all the time."

He sprang to her side, gently taking her arm in his hand. She lurched toward him ever so slightly. He felt the weight of her on his arm and marvelled that she was so much lighter than Phoebe.

"I'm not married, Nellie dear!" he cried. "It's not to be till Friday. You got the date wrong. And it won't be Friday, either. No, sir! I'm not going to let you go all the way out there alone. I said I'd look out for you when we were married, and I'm going to. You've got a husband, but what good is he to you? He's a brute. Yes, sir; I'm going with you and I don't give a cuss who knows it. See here! See this wad of bills? Well, by jingo, there's more than three thousand dollars there. I drew it out this morning to give to you if you were hard up. I——"

"Oh, Harvey, what a perfect fool you are!" she cried, tears in her eyes. "You always were a fool. Now you are a bigger one than ever. Go away, please! I can get along all right. Fairfax is paying for everything. Put that roll away! Do you want to be held up right here in the station?"

"And I've still got the photograph gallery," he went on. "It's rented and I get $40 a month out of it. I'll take care of you, Nellie. I'll see you safely out there. Then maybe I'll have to come back and marry old Mrs. Davis, God help me! I hate to think of it, but she's got her mind set on it. I don't believe I can get out of it. But she'll have to postpone it, I can tell you that, whether she likes it or not. Maybe she'll call it off when she hears I've eloped with another man's wife. She thinks I'm a perfect scamp with women, anyway, and this may turn her dead against me. Gee, I hope it does! Say, let me go along with you, Nellie; please do. You and I won't call it an elopement, but maybe she will and that would save me. And that beast of a Fairfax won't care, so what's the harm?"

"No," said Nellie, looking at him queerly. "Fairfax won't care. You can be sure of that."

"Then I'm with you, Nellie!" he shouted.

"You are a perfectly dreadful fool, Harvey," she said, huskily.

"I know it!" he exclaimed.

117